THE LAST VIAL

By
SAM McCLATCHIE, M. D.

I0541541

ARMCHAIR FICTION
PO Box 4369, Medford, Oregon 97504

*For more information about Armchair Books and products, visit our
website at…*

www.armchairfiction.com

Or email us at…

armchairfiction@yahoo.com

A NEW WORLD WAR?

The year was 1962. John McDonald was a veteran of the Korean War and now maintained a quiet career as a pathologist. Upon his return from a much-needed vacation, he found his co-workers struggling with the after-effects of a sudden and overwhelming flu epidemic that had struck the entire North American continent.

Careful analysis showed that this was no ordinary flu virus, but a man-made mutation that was unleashed on America's West Coast and quickly distributed across the continent.

Was it the communists, or someone else? Whoever it was, they had started a quiet but deadly game of germ warfare and it was up to the recently reinstated Colonel McDonald to find the perpetrators—and the antidote!

CAST OF CHARACTERS

DR. JOHN MCDONALD
All he wanted was a little quality time with his new love interest. Now they wanted him to save the world.

PAT DELANEY
She had no idea the world's future population would actually count on what she could achieve in her bedroom!

DR. GEORGE HALLAM
His was a position of great authority, but even that wouldn't convince those above him to listen—not without hard proof.

HARRY COPE
Not a tried and measured soldier, but he was all heart—and he had a huge score to settle with the Reds!

POLLY CRIPPS
She was Harry's fiancée, torn between the fear of losing him if he left, and the fear of what would happen if he stayed…

CAPTAIN BALAKIREFF
He was to lead his small Special Forces Unit into the very depths of Korean territory. Odds of getting them out? Slim.

ANDERS
This senior virologist was intimately involved in the Russians' world domination plot—but did his loyalties lie elsewhere?

1. And I heard a great voice out of the temple saying to the seven angels, "Go your ways and pour out the vials of the wrath of God upon the earth."

2. And the first went and poured out his vial upon the earth and there fell a noisome and grievous sore upon the men which had the mark of the beast and upon them which worshipped his image.
—Revelation 16

CHAPTER ONE

A LITTLE late, I pulled my Ferguson Cross-Country '62 into the space reserved for me and stepped out. The clouds were low and moving fast but the rain was soft on my bare grey head. The dark walls of the Laboratory rose close by. I felt the mass of it blocking off the light wind and, with the wind, the chill wetness of an autumn morning. It was good to be back, I thought, back to the quiet excitement of research, the prideful interest in my students, the comforting presence of my friends.

A female figure splashed by me hurriedly, her arms full of large brown envelopes. I half turned. "Lottie", I started to say...it was the Lab's messenger girl...but she was gone already "Funny", I mused, "she's usually ready to stop and chat at the least excuse." I turned back towards the Lab and almost collided with another woman, also loaded with what looked like case reports. "What the Hell!" I muttered to myself, but she was gone too. I quickened my pace, ran up the stone steps two at a time and passed through the big glass doors that open on the main hall of the Laboratory Building.

As the electronic eye closed them behind me I shrugged off my raincoat. I dropped a dime in the newsvendor and the paper popped up in its waterproof wrapper. The headline printed on the outside caught my eye as I started to shove it into my pocket. "New Epidemic Increases Hourly." New epidemic? What was the old one? Well, I'd find out soon enough. Maybe that explained Lottie and the case reports. I turned to go up the stairs to my office.

Behind the counter of the appointment desk Rosie, our senior receptionist, was watching me. Her bright black eyes and pert old face set under thick grey curls reminded me of a little bird curiously inspecting some strange new animal. Her high chirping voice completed the illusion.

"Good morning, Doctor Macdonald," she said and moved the sign on the arrival and departure board to show I was in.

"How was the vacation? Pat's in," she went on without waiting for an answer. "She says she ran into you a couple of times up in the Powell River Country."

I finished folding my raincoat before I looked at her.

"Yes, we did meet," I admitted cautiously but didn't explain further.

"I don't know how you manage that boat of yours all by yourself. Seems to me I'd want company to sail away up there in that rough water," she paused. "I hear Pat's a good sailor."

"You talk too damn much, Rosie," I growled and started along the hall. All the way up the stairs I remembered the twinkle in her eyes as I went past her.

The ground floor of the Laboratory is occupied by the Administration Office and Clinical Pathology Section. Shut off at the back are the white tiled walls and monel metal tables of the Autopsy Rooms. On the first floor the Tissue Pathologists sit at their microscopes and study the pretty blue and red stained slides of human and animal tissues, which come from the batteries of Technicon machines and the skillful microtomes of the laboratory technicians. Here too are the Medical Library and the Hematology Section, where blood from thousands of patients is smeared on slides, stained, and examined for signs of disease. I was just rounding the banister at the top of the stairs when, coming out of the Serology Room, I saw the long thin slow-moving figure and wavy blond hair of Harry Cope, the hematologist. He saw me at once and waved a languid hand.

"Hello, John! How was the holiday?" he said in his soft English voice.

"Pretty good, Harry. Keeping you busy?"

"Not in my own shop," he said. "But Dr. Hallam will certainly be glad to see you back. I've had to give him a hand the last day or two."

"Why, what's up?" I was surprised. Harry knew quite a bit about Virology and had kept up his interest in it even though hematology was his specialty. However he seldom worked for us unless there was a real emergency.

"I'd better let the Director tell you himself, old man. I have an appointment just now. See you later." He moved down the hall, as quiet and impassive as usual.

A little worried now, I went up the stairs to the second floor, passed Bacteriology and poked my head into the Virology Section. The routine work on virus diseases goes on here. The Research Lab, Dr. Hallam's pet project, is in a specially designed penthouse on the third floor, alongside the animal house, and is never used for ordinary tests.

In the Tissue Culture Room, Pat was already busy with the specimens and had time only to wink at me. No hope for enlightenment there! I looked back at her trim figure as I moved away and, at the door of Electron Microscopy, ran head on into Polly Cripps, our electron microscopy technician and Harry Cope's fiancée. Even at thirty-five she was still good looking in a bold way, with white gold hair waving over deep blue eyes, a full mouth and a full figure to go with it.

When I recovered my breath after bouncing off that pneumatic form, I started to speak but, as usual, she beat me to it.

"My Goodness, John, you Northerners are always in a hurry," she gasped. "You almost mashed me flat."

"Ah caint see no difference honey," I parodied her Alabama drawl. "Say, Harry tells me something big is happening."

"It surely is," she said, "I've taken more pictures in the last two weeks than in the six months before that. I took a whole mess of them to Dr. Hallam this morning."

"Maybe I'd better go find out for myself. See you later, cutie." As I went by I gave her a friendly pat on her well-rounded posterior and got the back of my head clipped for my temerity.

"You keep your cotton-pickin' hands to yourself, boy," she said, but she was smiling.

The time was late autumn. Because of a special project, I hadn't been able to take my summer vacation. Patricia Delaney, our senior virology technician, had worked with me and, as the days went by, it looked as if neither of us would get a break. The fall is the season for respiratory viruses to start causing trouble and we couldn't afford to take time off if even a minor outbreak appeared. But the weather stayed dry and finally, one lovely Indian summer day, Dr. Hallam had shoved us both out of the office for ten days' rest.

I stopped on the front steps of the Lab and looked at Pat, standing beside me, her brown curly head, topped by one of the new round space satellite hats, bent over as she fumbled at her handbag.

"Now what do we do?" I felt at a loss, a little tired and let down. I hadn't expected to get time off and consequently had made no plans for spending the next ten days. The sun was bright, the clouds were small and fluffy, the air was warm. It was autumn at its best. Surely it would be a shame to waste such wonderful weather.

Pat was speaking, her clear grey eyes thoughtful behind the heavy-rimmed glasses. The soft Louisiana voice was a treat after the harder northern accents of the Canadians.

"I don't know. I haven't made plans to do anything."

"Well then, let's go have some coffee and talk it over."

She nodded and fell into step beside me, her long legs, long for her medium height that is, keeping up with my short ones. In her high heeled shoes she stood as tall as I, her broad shoulders and slim but prettily rounded figure contrasting nicely with my stocky frame. We make a good pair, I thought, she, the American of Irish descent and I, the immigrant Irishman, educated in Canada and naturalized American during the Korean War. She had come to British Columbia just a year ago, when her marriage had broken up, to make a fresh start. The year before that I had returned to Canada to join the staff of the Civic Hospital as a pathologist.

We crossed the parking area to the main hospital building and went into the restaurant through the back entrance.

"How about this table?" I said and pulled out a chair for her. I tipped my head to the girl behind the counter and held up two fingers. The coffee came, not too strong, but at least it was hot. Pat shrugged out of her mackintosh, reached for the Players I held out to her and dragged at the battery match flame. I watched her as she leaned forward over the lighter. The tiny creases at the corners of her eyes, the slightly deeper lines of her mouth, marked her as a woman of thirty, mature, a little worldly, but still attractive. Delightfully so to me, I thought, since, at thirty-five and a casualty of the divorce mill too, I was no longer interested in young girls, good to look at but unseasoned by life.

She sat back in her chair and looked at me quizzically.

"Did I pass inspection?" she said.

I hadn't realized I'd been so obvious. It was a little disconcerting, even after dating her frequently in the last six months, to have my thoughts read the way she seemed to do.

I smiled at her. "I'll have to have a closer look to be sure."

"I don't know about that," she said teasingly. "I wouldn't trust you too far."

"How far would you trust me," I asked quickly, an idea growing hopefully behind my bantering tone.

She looked at me and her smile slowly faded. Again her intuition was right and the fear of getting emotionally tangled up with a man, the reluctance to bare her heart again so soon after it had been lacerated by another male, was obvious in her caution.

"It depends on what you want to do." She laid the cigarette down. It burned untouched as she watched my face.

"The satellite weather forecast is for good weather the next ten days," I said. "This looks like a perfect chance for a long cruise up the coast in my boat." I paused and looked straight at her, "but it takes two to work it properly."

She had been on one-day cruises with me before this and was learning quite quickly how to sail. I knew she would love to go but...

"Where do we stay at night?" she said.

"I didn't figure on any definite itinerary. We could sleep on the boat, there's plenty of room."

"I know that, but there's only one cabin."

"I won't bite you."

"Strictly platonic?"

"You call the tune, I'll play it." She stood up abruptly and reached out her hand to me. "We're wasting time," she said. "Let's go!"

I was thinking over those pleasant days and too platonic but still exciting nights as I came to the door of the Director's office. Dr. George Hallam, that straight backed old soldier, was sitting at his desk when I walked in. He was shuffling a pile of black and white photographs and, as they riffled over, I saw that they were some of Polly's electron microscope pictures of elementary particles. Hallam was a large man, but not fat, with black thinning hair combed straight back. Ordinarily a pleasant expression rested in the light brown eyes behind his rectangular spectacles, and a slight smile brightened his round, firm-fleshed face. Today he was definitely not happy, and under the white lab coat his big shoulders hunched forward determinedly like a fullback ready for a plunge through the line. I was wondering what bothered him until I caught a glimpse of the headlines in the "Sun" lying on the desk. EXTRA! Greatest Epidemic Fever! I noted the edition was later than the one I had bought. Flu Epidemic Spreads Through B.C. it said.

"Good morning, sir."

He nodded at me and I waved at the paper.

"What goes on since I left?"

"Five thousand cases of Flu."

Bang! He slapped the desk. "Just like that. In one day!" He ran one big hand over his chin and was silent, leaning on his elbows.

I picked up the paper to read the lead as he spoke again.

"That was a week ago. For three days the cases rose to a peak and then eased off. We've been working on it and I think we've isolated the virus." He looked up at me. "Didn't you know about it?"

"Chief," I said reproachfully, "You don't think I'd have stayed away if I'd known.

"No...no, of course not. I haven't had time to think much about it. But we could have used you and Pat. I'm damned glad you're back."

"We...ah...I didn't look at a paper for the whole time. Went for a trip in my boat. I even turned off the television."

"You must have had interesting company." He grinned at me slyly.

"Yeah, I had a good crew," I said and changed the subject. "But what about this epidemic?"

The fun died out of his eyes. "We've been expecting the second wave to hit anytime. Judging by the headlines we have it...and it's a corker. The Department of Health tells me it's spreading faster than a dirty story both north and south of the border."

"You say you have isolated it?"

He picked out several of the photographs and passed them across to me. I looked at them for a moment.

"But these particles are irregular, and too big!"

He nodded.

"What about the agglutination tests?"

"It isn't A, B or C," he said. "It's a new virus, or at least one I've never heard of. There doesn't seem to be a relationship to any other flu virus…and probably no immunity to it either."

"Then how do you know it is flu?"

"Only by the way it acts clinically. It fits the flu syndrome better than any other disease we can think of. Odd thing about this stuff," he mused, "as you can see, these first electron pictures don't look like flu and the Biochemistry Section also reports some unusual components in its chemical structure."

He stopped to light his pipe. "You remember how I broke up those simple plant viruses a few years ago and tried putting different pieces of them back together to make new ones?" He mumbled around his pipestem, blowing a little cloud of blue smoke with each word.

I hadn't been at the Civic at that time but I nodded in affirmation, not wanting to interrupt his train of thought.

"Well, this virus isn't the same of course, but it seems to be a relatively simple one and of such a peculiar composition it makes me wonder. Certainly, so far, it doesn't fit in with any of the natural viruses I've handled."

"Maybe it's an exotic variety brought in from overseas," I ventured. "Vancouver does handle a lot of foreign shipping. Or maybe it's a wild mutation from some ordinary flu virus. Look what happened in 1957 with that A prime mutation. Perhaps this thing has gone even farther away from the family tree."

"I thought of that but I'm not convinced." He shook his head in exasperation. "Damn it, man, there's something queer in this whole thing…and I can't put my finger on it!"

"What does the bug do to people, aside from the usual stuff?"

"They all get a sharp attack of the flu, lasting three or four days. The picture is typical as a rule, but on the mild side. Some of them act as if they had the mumps too."

"Hmm, that's nice," I said. "Has there been much orchitis in the male patients?"

"Who else could get it?" he gibed. "Now that you mention it, I believe there have been some cases," he said dryly, "but I've been more concerned with organic chemistry than with organs. By the way, how was your holiday?"

"The sly old dog," I thought. "He probably figures I've been having myself a time with Pat." Out loud I answered, "Just fine, Sir." I turned to go out. "Guess I'd better get started back to work. At least I got a good rest."

"Really, John, you call that a rest?" He was still chuckling as I shut the door behind me.

I changed to a white coat in my own small office. There was no definite job assigned to me now and I had no classes to teach this semester. I rambled around the office for a while, straightened out my desk and then decided to go down to Records and look up the case histories of the flu patients. It was partly idle curiosity but I knew that, sooner or later, the Old Man would have me working on it.

The girls in Records were full of questions about my vacation. That Pat and I were practically engaged was no secret, and the fact that someone had seen us together on my sloop was providing plenty of gossip.

"The hell with them," I thought. "Let them think what they want." At least it was not malicious gossip. We had a friendly crew in the Lab and the ribbing I was taking was all good-natured.

I went back to my office with a large bundle of case summaries loading me down. With the tremendous interest aroused in virology and the nature of protein molecules, because of the polio research of the Fifties, the drive to investigate the virus theory of cancer and the flu epidemic of 1957, a great deal of money had been spent to make the Civic Hospital a first class research center. Under Dr. Hallam's guidance and the sponsorship of the University of British Columbia, the Research Laboratory had become one of the best in North America. The Department of Health of B.C. cooperated enthusiastically in the fieldwork and I was able to get from our files the most detailed case histories prepared by their trained investigators. I spread out the charts, picked one at random, and began to study it.

Three hours later I was beginning to get the picture, at least up to date. Most of the cases gave a routine history. A few hours before the fever began they had noticed a mild head cold. This was followed by aching in the limbs and back, headache, fever, lack of appetite, and feeling generally ill and depressed. Some had swelling along the sides of their neck or under the chin, but that was not a prominent feature of their complaint. Several of the males also reported slight swelling of the testicles, less than is usually the case in mumps, and it did not seem to incapacitate them at all. The occasional female reported abdominal pains, which could have been due to inflamed ovaries, but it is difficult to make such a diagnosis with certainty. In inquiring about the movements of the patients before they became ill, the interrogators had turned up a few odd stories.

One woman reported that she had been standing in a crowded bus a few days before she got the flu when a man standing beside her had dropped a glass ball.

As she told it, "It looked like one of them souvenir things— you know, the kind that has a snowstorm inside it when you turn it upside down, or maybe it was a Christmas tree ornament. It broke just like you dropped a light bulb or somethin'. I thought I saw a kind of a cloud, like smoke, but it was only for a second. The man was nice about it, he apologized to me right away for scaring me. He was one of them D.P.'s I'm sure because he couldn't talk good English. That stuff that came out of it made my nose kinda itchy…made me sneeze. But I have hay fever and sinus, you know, had it for years. Maybe there was nothing to it."

The tape record of a male patient's report was also peculiar. I played it back, in part, on my own Dictape.

"I was sitting in the Automatic lunch, the big one on Granville. Well, it was full to the doors, just after twelve, and this guy comes in and gets a seat that another man had just left. He wasn't very tall but sort of husky and he reminded me of a guy I know who comes from Slovakia or one of them countries down in Europe. This guy, the friend of mine I mean, he works for Baden Brothers in the Foundry... Yeah, yeah, I'm getting to the point in a minute. Well, as I was telling you, this fella who looks like my friend has a pile of parcels and he's trying to manage a cup of coffee at the same time so I give him a hand...I'm just about finished with my pie. We get the parcels down O.K. but he upsets one of the bags with his foot on the floor. I start to pick it up and he tries to beat me to it. These guys from Europe fall all over themselves to be polite. Anyway he grabs an insect bomb that fell out and somehow, I can't for the life of me figure it, he gets the thing stuck and the spray starts to go out all over the place. We couldn't shut it off but it didn't last long. He told me it was a new kind—good for one time only, so it was made cheap. I dunno if that stuff had anything to do with this flu but I know it made my nose itch for a while. Maybe that did it...I knew a guy one time that..."

I shut off the tape and turned to another report.

"I was in the Paramount," she said, "watching that new Tri-Di movie they call *High Time*...it's a sort of a Western and musical all mixed up. It's a real good movie but that three-dimensional stuff scares you when they show a fight. I don't think that's too good for little kids, do you? It was the part where the hero, what's his name, oh yeah, Bert Blaine, is getting romantic with Nellie Golding just before he rides away to catch the killer. It's kinda sad too and all of a sudden my eyes started to water. Well, I'm sentimental, you know, but I don't cry that easy and anyhow I hadn't felt like crying just yet if you know what I mean. It was more like an itch. I looked around in the dark to see what might be wrong and then I noticed a hissing noise like a radiator leaking. I leaned over to ask the man in the next seat if he heard it too but right about then it stopped and he got up and left. I don't know how he could have anything to do with it but I know my eyes and nose were itchy for a long time. I'll just tell you that I must have got the flu from that. My mother says that's nonsense but I don't care."

The rest of the reports were routine. Some noted exposure to colds but none to mumps. The three unusual stories I dismissed as having no real connection with the epidemic. Aerosol sprays of all shapes and sizes are so common nowadays that they are used in every kind of commodity which can be packed that way. I know of no disease caused by the gases they contain unless it be allergy to the various insecticides and other chemicals spread by the gases. People often have peculiar ideas as to what starts a cold. The statisticians had run off the figures, including the odd possibilities, on the Minicalculator at the Department of Health and their report stated there was no significance in such stories. So I guess that settled that in this mathematically minded era. Sometimes I wish that medicine were the art it used to be instead of the statistical science it has become. But I never did like mathematics.

Shortly after noon I gave up and strolled down to the Culture Room, looking for Pat. I found her busy with a dentist's drill, in the old fashioned way, cutting holes in the shells of fertilized eggs and transferring virus cultures from old eggs to new. Between the cap and mask only her cool grey eyes were visible, intent on the thin membranes that pulsated above the tiny heart of the young chicken. Her fingers were quick and sure as she injected the virus then released the opening with scotch tape, or sometimes with a glass coverslip, sealed around the edges with Vaseline. Hallam wasn't too keen on the new short wave cutter and plastic film technique. When she paused for a moment to flame her needles I rapped on the glass partition to catch her attention and then made eating signs. She nodded and, a few minutes later, we sat over sandwiches and coffee in the hospital restaurant.

"How did the morning go?" she said, finishing her sandwich and starting on a second cup of coffee.

"The old man was needling me the way you needle those eggs of yours," I grumbled. "We don't have the private life of goldfish around here. The girls were hinting for information too."

"What do you expect," she laughed. "After all, you're the most eligible bachelor in the place."

I wandered over to the counter for a pack of Exports. The noon Sun was out and I saw the lead story. "Flu Epidemic Disorganizes Seattle, Tacoma, Portland." I bought the paper and went back to Pat.

"We're not much ahead of the news hawks," was all she said.

As we passed the front office, on the way back to Virology, Rosie waved at me.

"Dr. Macdonald, you're wanted in the Conference Room right away. And you too, Pat! There's some sort of big pow-wow. Tissue Path., Biochem., Bacteriology, Public Health, and all the clinical services too!"

"O.K. Thanks, Rosie," I said.

We went on up the stairs. The Director didn't like the elevators used, except for freight, so we all had to walk. Probably it was better for us too, I thought; comparing the slight shortness of breath I noticed on second floor with the way I'd hiked over the hills around Kumwha during the Korean truce talks of 1951, when there was nothing to do in my Battalion Aid Station but take morning sick call. But I'd sat in a lot of chairs since then.

The Conference Room, next to Dr. Hallam's office, was already crowded and he waved at us. "John, you find a spot somewhere along the wall. I'm afraid we can't seat everyone and I want department heads at the table. Pat, would you mind taking notes? Sit here beside me." He winked at her. "That is, if John trusts me."

The few remaining spaces were now filled and the Director stood up.

"Gentlemen, some of you know why I have arranged this meeting but the rest of you are still wondering. You may or may not agree with what I shall have to say, but, because of its unusual nature, I must have your promise that you will not repeat, outside of this room, what you will hear in the discussion that follows. Is that clear?" He paused and looked around the room. "Anyone who does not wish to give such a promise will please leave now, before we start."

I could see their faces from where I stood by the windows. Joe Armstrong, Chief of Medical Services, sat on Hallam's right. His dark, heavy-featured face was calm as he looked straight ahead. He knows, I thought. Beside him, Bruce Thompson, Chief of Surgery, lifted his bushy eyebrows and turned to whisper a quick question at Joe. Obviously he didn't know the secret, whatever it was. I looked on around the table. About halfway, I saw Ray Thorne, one of the best obstetricians in town and an old friend of mine. He caught my eye and winked. The Chief of Ob. and Gyn. wasn't there. Ray must be standing in for him. I wondered what the boss would have to say that could interest their department.

Hallam was talking again. "About a week ago, here in Vancouver there was a sudden outbreak of disease which, aside from a few unusual occurrences, seemed to be influenza. Now, in the past two days, we are confronted with thousands of new cases. You have seen the reports in the newspapers, I'm sure. I have been in contact with the public health authorities here, and also in the States of Washington and Oregon. The situation down there, especially in Seattle, Tacoma and Portland, is every bit as bad as it is here." He paused for a full five seconds. "Gentlemen, I believe this is no ordinary epidemic. I believe this may well be a man-made disaster!"

"For the love of God, George!" I don't know who said it, but it echoed all our thoughts. I could see the astonished and incredulous looks on the faces of all the experts as they watched him, standing there so straight and solid and sane.

My mind was racing about, trying to find reasons for his amazing assertion. Maybe he wasn't really serious, I thought, only to dismiss the idea immediately. Another look at that stern and sober face and I knew he meant it. And only a few moments ago he had been laughing and joking with Pat. I remembered a story I'd heard about him in World War II, how he had been in a Field Hospital with his New Zealand countrymen at Cassino and, during a heavy bombardment, had sat quietly joking with patients who could not be moved to safety. So, it could be true. If he could make jokes in the face of death, he could laugh during a disaster.

The buzz of conversation ceased as the Chief went on. "As of this morning there were fifty thousand cases in Vancouver city alone, with no tallies in, as yet, from Burnaby and New Westminster. More are being reported every minute. The hospitals are filling up even though they take only those with complications; and there seems to be no end of it so far. It's like the 1918 pandemic all over again but with some very peculiar differences." Again he stopped and turned to Dr. Armstrong. "Joe, do you see any differences clinically?"

Armstrong got to his feet. "Yes, I do, George," he said, in his slow careful way. "For one thing, it is the most explosive epidemic I have ever seen. Usually they start with a few cases and, after an incubation period of two or three days, a fresh batch of victims appears, growing in number each time. Here we have hundreds, all at once, then none for about five days or so, then thousands. It does look almost as if something or somebody had infected them all at the same time."

"My God," I thought, "not you too, Joe! Not old steady-boy down-to-earth Armstrong! Shades of the flying saucers!"

He continued. "The time lapse between the first outbreak and this new surge of cases is approximately five days, which is just a little longer than usual for influenza. Also, as Dr. Hallam has already mentioned, there are some peculiarities in the clinical picture. For instance, we are seeing patients with enlargement of the salivary glands...not many of course...and a few with orchitis. We even have the occasional female with what could be inflammation of the ovaries. That makes me think of mumps except that the time between the first and second waves is much too short, and anyway most of these people tell me they had mumps as a child."

One of the public health men down the table broke in. "I remember back in 1956 there was some sort of epidemic pleurisy, or Q-fever, in California, in which there were cases with involvement of the salivary and sex glands. It was quite an unusual thing but I don't remember the outcome. And there were miscarriages in the '57 flu epidemic, so the ovaries were probably involved in some cases. Nobody can say those weren't natural epidemics."

"Yes, that sort of thing does happen from time to time," Armstrong agreed. "We have to postulate a mutation in the virus. Even today we haven't classified them completely and this one could be a new variety with an odd life cycle. There's one good thing about this," he concluded, "although it seems to be far more infectious than anything we've ever seen before, it isn't anything like as dangerous as the 1918 flu, or even the 1957 pandemic. We haven't had anyone die yet. Most of them are well in three or four days after the fever begins. Maybe that's because we have the antibiotics to take care of the secondary bacterial invasion. That's what caused most of the pneumonia and all the other complications that killed so many people in 1918. Frankly I'm not worried, even though I talked it over with George, here, before the meeting. I think probably everyone will get it since people who have had the ordinary types of flu or flu shots do not appear to be immune. But it's no worse than a cold. When almost everybody has had it, it will die out. I don't agree with Dr. Hallam. I think it is a natural epidemic."

He sat down, the tension in the room already eased by his calm and sensible summary of the facts.

"What do you say to that, George?" Thompson sliced the silence with his question in the same decisive manner as he made his surgical incisions.

The Chief smiled at him. "Right now I can't prove a thing, Bruce. All that I have is suspicion...call it a hunch if you will.

That's why I don't want any loose talk. The whole pattern of this epidemic, and of the virus that seems to be the cause, is foreign to my experience. The electron microscope pictures that we have, so far, show a particle that is different in shape and size to our known influenza viruses, and to any other ordinary disease virus. Our serological tests don't identify it. The Biochemistry Section has been working on it twenty-four hours a day. As yet they haven't got too far, but far enough to show that there are definite differences in the molecular pattern between this virus and influenza, as we know it. It seems to be a simpler than usual pattern, reminiscent of the synthetic viruses we made some years ago. There are some amino acid groupings like those of the mumps virus too, which could possibly account for its affinity for the salivary glands. I think it will prove able to transmit its characteristics indefinitely from one generation to the next—it has, so far. We have it growing in chick embryos right now but it's to soon to be definite about anything. If it continues to transmit all its characteristics, that would be a possible argument against my theory that this is a man-made epidemic." He paused for a sip of water from the glass in front of him.

"Would you care to elaborate on your theory?" Smith, the tissue pathologist interrupted, his long narrow chin thrust forward and his deep-set eyes intent on the speaker.

"Be glad to, Tom," Hallam agreed. "I believe this is a man made epidemic, as I said before. The timing is too orderly, too sudden, to be natural. I suspect, because of its unusual structure, especially the resemblance to previous experimental viruses, that this is a synthetic virus, made up either from relatively simple chemical compounds or perhaps from particles of natural viruses recombined in a different pattern. As you all know, it has been possible for years now to take a virus apart, so that it will not reproduce, and then put these parts together again, not from the same culture, but just as if you took parts of a motor from the stock bins and assembled an engine. When it is reassembled with parts similar to the ones it was originally made up of, it will reproduce again just like the natural virus. We have also been able to crystallize many viruses and then start them growing again by putting the crystals in the proper nutrient solutions. Recently it has been possible to combine amino acids and other chemicals into simple forms that act much like viruses but are not quite the same. But there is one obstacle that we have not yet overcome. Whether we have recombined different parts of various viruses or whether we have made up amino acid combinations, it has not been possible to have this synthetic virus transmit all its characteristics from generation to generation. It breaks up; it is not stable."

"But you all know this." He stopped to light a cigarette, gathering his thoughts as he watched the end glow. He exhaled little gusts of smoke as he spoke again. "As far as I can tell now, this virus is unchanged through each passage in the egg, which might put it out of the synthetic class. Mutations have been induced artificially by using chemicals such as the sulfonamides to interfere with the lifecycle. This has turned some disease viruses into harmless types, but, unless the Americans in their Biological Warfare Center have done it, and they aren't talking of course, the reverse is not true. Certainly I know of nobody in the democratic world who has made such a virus."

There was no mistaking his emphasis. Again Smith spoke up.

"Are you implying that the Communists may have produced such a virus?"

The answer came slowly. Hallam was frighteningly serious now.

"Yes, I believe it is possible. In the last few years there has been a tremendous amount of research on viruses and nucleoproteins in Russia. Kaganovich and his associates have published some very advanced work on the synthesis of proteins and Magidoff is an outstanding virologist by any standards."

"Ay, that's true." Ian Gordon, the little sandy haired biochemist burst out in his broad Scots brogue. "And I wouldna think they've been puttin' out all they know either, if I'm to judge from what they said at the last International Conference in Stockholm."

"But where's the point in all this?" Joe Armstrong exclaimed. "This stuff isn't deadly; it isn't even serious, now we have the antibiotics to prevent complications. As a secret weapon it could have no more than nuisance value. Personally, I think old George may be chasing something red, but it will turn out to be a red herring instead of a Communist."

There were smiles all around the table. Even Hallam grinned. He and Joe had been great friends and sparring partners for years.

Joe went on, "I believe this is just one of those wild mutations that crop up occasionally and cause big epidemics. True, I can't explain the amazing suddenness of its onset, but to call it bacteriological warfare is just ridiculous."

"I can't deny what Joe says, but he can't prove I'm wrong either," Hallam retorted. "I hope I am but I wanted you all to know what I think so you will keep alert for any evidence for or against my theory. On the face of it, as Joe says, it seems ridiculous that any enemy would bother with such a harmless weapon. But it could be a trial run for something much worse. I have tried to keep my emotions out of my appraisal of the facts and when I do I still say that this thing is not natural. Once more I would remind you not to talk about this outside. It could start up a lot of trouble. That's all, thank you, gentlemen."

I was going out at the tail end of the crowd when the Chief lifted his chin at me in the come-hither sign. I stayed. Pat stayed too when he put a restraining hand on her shoulder.

"I suppose you think I'm way out on a limb, John," Hallam said quizzically.

"Frankly, sir, I thought Joe Armstrong had already sawed it off."

"Then I take it you aren't in favor of the virus warfare idea."

"Well, I did get a bit tired of B.W. talk in the U.S. Army. Down in the States they scare little kids with the word red, but after a while it loses its shock value."

"You'll have to admit this is a very unusual epidemic," he countered.

"True, but as Dr. Armstrong said, what possible purpose is there?" I lifted my shoulders and turned up my palms to emphasize my doubt. "Suppose the Reds are responsible. They wouldn't do it just to annoy us and I doubt if they would make a trial run in North America before letting the real disease loose. They are much too cautious for that."

"Maybe we haven't found the real reason," Pat broke in. "If this virus is the weapon it must be doing something that hasn't shown up yet…some long term effect."

"I think you've hit it, Pat," Hallam brightened up again. "And that's why I kept you two back here. I want you and John to drop everything else and work with me up in the Research Lab. We'll run a series of tests on our experimental animals until we find out what this virus really does. It may be too late by then to do anything about it but we must work night and day until that time comes. There's plenty of food in the penthouse kitchen. I got it stocked up yesterday. And we will have to use the bedrooms too, if Pat doesn't mind sleeping up there at night with two handsome chaps like you and me." He ogled her like the villain of an old melodrama.

"But sir," she said, playing her part, "I've never slept three in a bed before. Isn't it crowded?"

"Maybe we can arrange to push John out," he laughed. "But let's get up there now. There's no time to lose."

CHAPTER TWO

WHEN the Pathology Lab was being built, Dr. Hallam had insisted on a completely separate Research Unit on the third floor. It sat up there, next to the Animal House, a part of which connected with it, and with it alone, so that even the animals were isolated. The unit itself contained a complete set of the most modern equipment used in virology, equipment that was never touched except on Hallam's order. To prevent outside contamination and also to prevent the escape of harmful diseases, all who wanted to go into the unit had to put the clothes they were wearing into the ultra-sound sterilizer locker, take a complete shower and, in a dressing room where the blue rays of ultraviolet light killed more germs, put on white suits. Naturally anyone with a cold or other obvious disease was barred. All clothes needed for a long stay were processed through the ultra-sound locker and picked up on the other side of the shower room. These precautions were sufficient only for entry to the Penthouse as Hallam had christened the living quarters. They consisted of a pleasant, if austere suite containing bedrooms, bathrooms, kitchen and living room, where those who were working on a project would stay for days at a time. To get into the workrooms, it was necessary to wear what looked like modified space suits, which contained their own oxygen supply, and go through a chemical shower guaranteed to kill any living organism. Many of the experimental animals had been delivered at birth by special aseptic techniques and they and their descendants lived in air-conditioned rooms where the only germs were those introduced deliberately in experiments. Other animals, which were unsterile, were kept in separate rooms and handled by remote control devices as if they were pieces of radioactive material...and some of them were, with injections of isotopes coursing through their blood. Even their feeding and cleaning was handled by remote control, by assistants especially trained for the task. At this particular time all other special work was stopped or transferred to the Routine Lab. The Research Unit was cleaned and waiting for us.

Hallam and I went through the shower routine first and then sat waiting at the table in the living room for Pat. She came in soon afterwards, her cheeks shining from scrubbing and her pink lips devoid of lipstick, smiling as she tried to tie up her hair with a towel.

"Gracious, that needle shower is rough," she said. "I've scrubbed so hard I must surely be sterile."

"I hope not, baby," I said. "I've got plans for your future."

"Really, John, sometimes you go too far." She blushed as Hallam laughed.

"What do we do now, Chief?" I said.

"I'm not particularly interested in trying to find out the structure of this virus," Hallam said. "We'll let Biochemistry and the Routine Lab people handle that. I've warned them to be particularly careful. What I should like to do up here is to find out if the virus has any hidden power...if it does more to people than just give them the flu. The thing that bothers me is the time element. Right now nobody is really worried. I have to find enough evidence to convince the government so they'll do something. We'll keep passing the virus through chicken embryos...we know it can be kept alive that way; and we'll put it in Hela cells and any other tissue culture we have, both human and animal. They aren't ordinarily suitable for flu virus but with this thing one can't tell."

He turned to me. "How many ferrets have we?"

"I can't say exactly, I haven't been here since my vacation. But there were plenty."

"And monkeys?"

"Do you want them for monkey kidney culture, or what?"

"No, I want to give them the flu and then see what happens. It could affect ferrets in a different way than human beings. We can't use people so it has to be monkeys."

"Well, we have more than a dozen, if we take all varieties."

"That'll do nicely. Pat, you might start on mice after you inoculate a fresh batch of eggs. John and I will tackle the ferrets and monkeys. They're difficult for one person to handle easily. And we'll do hamsters and guinea pigs too. Something ought to show up in a day or two."

Hours later it was finished. It isn't the easiest job in the world to inoculate ferrets and monkeys with virus, especially when it had to be put in their noses. Those nasty little weasels can bite and even through the puncture proof gloves I felt the pinch when one of them got loose. The monkeys weren't much better. Finally, covered with sweat inside my suit, I came back through the chemical shower, the water shower and the dryer and opened the headpiece for a breath of fresh air.

"You'd think they could have air-conditioned these damn suits," I grumbled. "Say Pat, when do we eat?"

Pat had just got the helmet off and was fluffing her brown curls, flattened down by the green surgeon's cap she had been wearing underneath it.

"Just as soon as you leave and let me get out of this diver's suit," she said.

Hallam winked at me as he opened the door. "Too bad these suits aren't transparent."

We were sitting around the table over the remains of steak and french fries when the midnight news reports came over the TV. There was nothing more to do at the moment; the animals were not yet sick even though we were hoping for a much shorter incubation period in the ferrets than in monkeys or man. It had to be shorter if we were going to do anything in time.

"First the British Columbia news," the announcer was saying. "We now have reports of outbreaks of influenza in the Interior. Kamloops has several hundred cases. Kelowna and Princeton hospitals are full. Across the border, Yakima and Spokane report a similar situation."

Hallam cut in. "There it is again. A sudden explosive outburst! It's not right, I tell you. It's not natural!"

"We now turn to the international scene." A brightly colored map of Europe appeared on the screen and, as the announcer spoke, he pointed. "Here, in the West German Republic, there are reports of an influenza epidemic that may be similar to ours. Apparently the Communists in the new country of Prussia, until recently called East Germany, feel it is serious. They have closed the border. An airlift to Berlin is beginning and the West Germans have requested the return of American and British transports to their old bases since their own air fleet is insufficient for the task. There are scattered reports from Yugoslavia which may indicate an epidemic there too, but the Tito government refuses to confirm this." He paused and the picture shifted to a map of the Far East. "Over in the Orient we have a different story. For the past several weeks there have been persistent rumors of a strange disease ravaging Tibet and West China. Communications are poor, of course, and the Chinese Communists have not authorized any official announcement. However, it is said that the disease has some resemblance to small pox. Other travelers insist it is more like a severe hemorrhagic measles. All agree that the mortality is high and that the already inadequate medical services of the Chinese, in those areas, are overwhelmed. The Russians are reported to be flying antibiotics to the Peiping government, but claim that they are having scattered outbreaks in Siberia which require their attention. They admit closing all frontier posts, ostensibly in an effort to prevent the spread of the disease."

I looked at Hallam. "Now what?"

He made a face. "My word! This complicates things, doesn't it? Not only are there two epidemics but the Reds have the worst one. If the reports are true, this Asiatic outbreak could be worse than the Black Death of the Middle Ages."

The TV had returned to reporting the local scene in detail.

"It is now ten days since the first cases of influenza appeared. The second big wave of cases is now passing its peak, the authorities believe, but we are getting thousands more cases scattered all over the city and the outlying metropolitan areas of New Westminster, Burnaby, North and West Vancouver. According to the Department of Public Health, this distribution suggests a disease of extremely high infectivity with about a five-day cycle. However they also say there is no cause for alarm. Even though the number of cases is well into the hundreds of thousands, practically no deaths have been reported. What deaths there are have invariably been old people or those whose strength has been weakened by other illness."

He continued for a time but said nothing new and Hallam shut him off.

Pat stood up. "If you all are going to keep your promise and clean up the dishes, I'll take a look in the viewing window and see how our pets are coming along. Then I'm going to bed."

I groaned in dismay. "Now let's not make a habit of this. I hate doing dishes!"

She pulled my left ear as she went by. "Do you good. You need the practice!"

"All right, John," said the Chief. "I'll wash and you dry. I should have installed an automatic dishwasher in this place. Didn't think of it at the time."

I'd just dried the first plate when the Intercom buzzed. I pushed the button.

"Dr. Hallam! John! Can you come up right away? I think things are starting to pop." She sounded excited and a bit puzzled.

The big man lifted his eyebrows and rinsed off his hands.

"I guess we'd better get over there," he said, mangling my tea towel to get the water off.

When we reached the viewing room we found Pat, completely engrossed, in the section which overlooked the cages containing the female ferrets. It was a one-way glass, and soundproof, as the weasel tribe are notoriously sensitive to outside disturbances. Pat pointed to one of the cages and said in an unnecessary whisper.

"That ferret is sick. She seems to be in labor."

"It's a good old ferret custom," I quipped.

"Idiot!" She frowned impatiently. "According to her chart, she was only in the early part of pregnancy...not due for a long time yet. She was the first one you inoculated today."

For a while longer we watched. There was no doubt about it. The ferret was aborting. I glanced at the Chief. His face was set, the normally gentle mouth was grim, the lips drawn and thin.

"God Almighty," he whispered. "They wouldn't try it. And yet, what better way?" He straightened up from his seat. Even now he couldn't resist a mild joke.

"When you say things are popping, young lady, I see you mean it literally."

He started for the exit. "Well, it appears that the real work is beginning. I'd hope we would all get some sleep but the flu virus works too fast in these ferrets. So let's go back for some coffee and see what happens."

Bacon and eggs certainly taste good after a long night, I was thinking as I champed into the last piece of toast. I got it down, drained my glass of powdered milk and held up my coffee cup to Pat. She looked tired, a little pale, from lack of sunlight, perhaps, and very thoughtful as she filled it. I touched her hand as the cup passed back to me and she smiled tenderly. If Hallam saw it, he made no comment. I felt sorry for him at times like that. He was, in spite of his friendliness, a lonely man. I remembered now that his fiancée, an Army nurse, had been killed at Cassino in the unit he commanded. Since that time he had turned to his work for consolation and apparently had never found anyone he really cared for.

"Sir," I said—somehow I never could bring myself to use his first name; habit is strong and he looked too much like a soldier even now, a soldier who commanded respect. "Sir, what did you mean last night, as that ferret was aborting, when you said they wouldn't try it, and yet what better way?"

"I suppose to explain that, I'd better give you my reasoning in this whole business." He looked at his watch. "We've an hour before the next stage of our experiments...not enough to sleep. At any rate we can sleep later."

Pat refilled the cups and silently I passed around a packet of Sweet Caps. He lit one and started.

"As you both remember, after Stalin died there was a period of uncertainty and then, when Malenkov gave way to the Krushchev-Bulganin team, the so-called Geneva conference-at-the summit initiated what has been called the peace offensive by the Russians. The Hungarian revolt and the trouble in East Germany and Poland put a crimp in their pious front. That front was still further dinted by their obvious interference in the Middle East. But aside from that, the uneasy truce has continued, mainly, I suppose, because of the fear of an H-bomb war. Except for Tibet, Red China too has been fairly quiet, mostly because she still doesn't have the industrial potential to fight a major war; and the Soviets have procrastinated in helping her because they, too, fear the dreadful potential of such a population, if armed."

"The Geophysical Year saw both Russian and American satellites circling the world and the race for the Intercontinental Ballistic Missile, with H-bomb warhead, seems to have ended in a stalemate. The Russians, the Yanks, and now the British Commonwealth, possess long-range rockets of great accuracy. The next logical step, since both atomic and ballistic wars promise mutual suicide, is into space. There, the two main opponents could spy on each other and neither the Iron Curtain nor the security regulations of the USA would hide secret preparations for a knockout punch. Also, there possibly are immense stores of valuable minerals open to the owners of the moon and planets. But space travel takes time and money...and brains. Manned satellites are on the way, but are not yet established facts."

"The Sputniks of 1958 had shaken the States out of its complacency as nothing else could. By 1961, therefore, that country had reversed its trend in favor of labor and the common man and at last had recognized that it was the uncommon man who had enabled it to achieve its tremendously high material standards. They were catching up very rapidly with the Russians, who for a time had had a preponderance of scientific personnel, and had managed, by sacrificing consumer goods to heavy industry, to keep ahead of the States in the machinery of war. With a stalemate, at least temporarily, in science, the Americans turned back to economic warfare. For a time the Reds, with their lavish promises, had been ahead in this field too, but the deliveries of goods didn't match the promises and gradually disillusionment had set in. So the Americans, who could be depended upon to deliver the goods, gradually forged ahead. As it now stands, they are slowly but certainly pushing the Communists out of all but the captured satellite countries and even there, the years of repression and low standards of living have resulted in several serious revolts in the past ten years. Then too, in educating their people in the attempt to achieve scientific supremacy, the Communists have awakened them to the fallacies of the Marxist-Leninist doctrines.

"Now dictators seldom give up quietly. The Commies are strained to the limit and in danger of losing. They have to do something—but they aren't fools. You can't have atomic war without suicide. Local wars and political maneuvering have failed. They are losing the economic war. There is only one answer!"

Deliberately he paused to let the argument sink in…a favorite habit of his.

"A new kind of war! That's the answer! A war that is over before anyone realizes it has started—and a war that cannot be blamed on them, so there is no danger of retaliation."

He drew hard on his cigarette, butted it firmly, and went on.

"I believe that this present epidemic has been started by enemy agents. I further believe that it is due to a synthetic virus, which combines the terrific contagiousness of the 1918 flu with certain features of mumps, and perhaps German measles. I think the virus has been built up in such a way that there is no cross immunity with any natural virus; in other words, having had mumps or flu or shots for either will be no protection. And, to make it even more diabolical, they have deliberately made it a mild type of infection so that almost everyone gets better, and people are therefore not concerned about it. As Joe Armstrong said, the stuff isn't serious. So why suspect sabotage until it is too late."

"But the Russians themselves are reporting cases," I said, "and how do you explain this pandemic in Red China that's killing off so many people. That is an entirely different disease."

"I agree," Hallam said thoughtfully, "and that's the beauty of the whole plan. If you learn to make one virus that transmits its characteristics, you should be able to make others. A killer virus let loose in North America would alarm the entire continent overnight. Our public health people would isolate whole cities, if necessary, and probably eliminate it before it got out of hand. We have no quarantine for this epidemic. Nobody is worried about it and many authorities feel if a big epidemic cannot be controlled by their inadequate medical staff they might as well be killed off now."

"You mean the Soviets want to eliminate the Chinese too?" Pat was incredulous.

"Yes, I do." The Chief nodded emphatically. "They want to rule the whole world, not just a part of it. As time goes by, the Chinese are more and more of a threat to their supremacy. That threat must be eliminated."

"What about reports of flu and the new small pox thing in Russia and Siberia?" I asked.

He was almost enthusiastic. "It's a lovely plan. Yes, lovely, if it weren't so horrible in its implications." He paused to drain his cup. "For the past several years there has been very strong emphasis on public health measures in the USSR. A tremendous drive for vaccination against polio, small pox and various other communicable diseases has resulted in the immunization of millions of children and adults. I'll bet if we could get some of those vaccines we'd find the antidote to both our flu virus and the Chinese small pox-measles, whatever it is. I think there has been deliberate selection of part of the population to carry on the Soviet system and the rest will be sacrificed just to fool us. After all, the Reds believe in genetics as we do, now that Lysenko and his theories are discredited, and what more logical than breeding a better race?"

"I'm not quite sure I follow that last part," I said. "Only the Chinese are being killed off."

"Only the Chinese are dying, as individuals," Hallam spoke slowly and emphatically, "but I fear we are also dying—as a nation!"

CHAPTER THREE

THE sloop bucked a little as the bow chopped into a wave and fell a few points off course. The steady chugging of the small marine engine pushed her on, sidling up over the low rollers and sliding down the other side joyfully like a little kid on a playground coaster. The wind was cool and gentle, the sun bright in the southeast. We were running north, close to the coast, with Bowen Island and Gibsons already far astern. At that time of year, and in the middle of the week, traffic was light. The nearest ship was only a smudge on the horizon. I bent a line around the tiller and went below.

In the starboard bunk Pat lay sleeping quietly. A light breeze from the port floated a wisp of hair and dropped it back on her forehead with each lift of the bow. I bent over and kissed her gently on the mouth. She smiled faintly in her sleep and her arms came up around my neck as she began to wake up. I disengaged them gently.

"Go back to sleep darling. It's not time for your watch yet."

I straightened the covers over her, and went into the tiny galley.

The coffee was hot and the eggs I had set on the stove previously were boiling. I sat down to eat. The Benzedrine I had taken to keep me going all through the night was wearing off. I could feel the faint quivering of fatigue in my arms and legs. My eyes were dry and burning a little. In two or three hours I could wake Pat and get some sleep myself. In the meantime all I had to do was to steer the sloop north, towards one of our favorite islands, a small, uninhabited, rock and tree covered hump where we could be alone to rest and relax.

And as I ate quickly and quietly, as I cleaned up the dishes and went back on deck, the words of Dr. Hallam kept running through my head like a squirrel through a maze, darting and searching for the answer. "Only the Chinese are dying as individuals, but I fear we are dying as a nation!"

I had sat there, flabbergasted, my mouth open like a moron, the incredible statement echoing through the suddenly empty chambers of my brain.

"The ferret..." Pat spoke through the horror-stiffened fingers that clawed at her mouth. Her eyes stared widely at the deliberately composed features of the director.

"Yes, my dear...the ferret."

"Oh, no... Oh, God no not now!" It was not a cry of anguish for the world but something personal, deeper, a cry of despair.

"What's all the fuss about?" I said crossly. "I don't get it." I turned to Pat. "What're you having a hissy about?"

Hallam looked at me with patient resignation.

"If you were a woman you'd be having a hissy too, as you call it."

"That's her word for it sir," I said. "If you two are all up in the air because a ferret has an abortion I can't see why. There are plenty of diseases that affect animals differently to man. What about undulant fever? It causes abortion in cattle but doesn't affect pregnant women any more than many other serious diseases do. So a ferret drops its kittens! So it might have done it equally with any other high fever."

"You're quite right John," Hallam said, "but remember, this is no ordinary disease. This is a secret weapon and, if it does cause miscarriages and perhaps permanent damage to the ovaries, the result will be a catastrophe for the West."

"Doggone it, Chief, if you'll pardon my saying so, you're getting positively paranoid about this whole business. We haven't a shred of real evidence so far."

"Again you're right, but this is one time where intuition and a high index of suspicion should prevail over cool scientific detachment. We haven't got time for a series of controlled experiments. We've got to guess, and guess right!"

"He's right, John!"

"OK Pat, OK! Trot out your woman's intuition and we'll all fly off into the wild blue yonder. I only hope we don't come down with a dull thud."

"All the ferrets are snuffling with the flu," Hallam said. "It's unfortunate that only one was pregnant, otherwise we might have had confirmation of our hunch by now."

"I haven't heard of any increase in miscarriages among pregnant women who got the flu," I said. "To me that's pretty good evidence that the bug doesn't affect human beings that way. For that matter, there were more reports of testicular involvement than of ovarian disease."

"If it does affect pregnant women, maybe it affects the fetus. Maybe children will be born deformed like the cases of German measles in early pregnancy," Pat said.

"That's a gruesome thought," I said. "You two give me the creeps this morning." I looked at my watch. "Lord it's five o'clock! This has been a rough session."

"And not finished yet," groaned Hallam, pushing up out of his chair. "Only the ferrets are sick so far. We'll sacrifice a few females...and some males too. Send them down to Smith for examination. He has a doctor and technicians on twenty-four hour duty and they can get cracking right away. Tell him to concentrate on glandular tissues, with first priority for the sex glands. And get cultures from the usual tissues before you send them down."

"Will do," I said, and left the room.

I was back in half an hour. Both Pat and Dr. Hallam came into the living room shortly afterwards.

"None of the other animals show any sign of illness yet," Pat said. "We'll have to wait a little longer."

"Look, I don't think anything will happen for the next twenty-four hours," the chief said. "Why don't you two buzz off. Relax all you can. There's a busy time coming and you won't be able to get out again for a while. It's early…you could get down to the boat and go for a sail. Keep away from people; I don't want you catching the flu. Come back early tomorrow morning so nobody will be around."

"What about you?" Pat and I said it together.

"I'll get some sleep now and then putter around and read until I hear from Smith."

"Smith was there himself. He said he would do some frozen sections as well as the usual paraffin."

"In that case I shall have some more toast and coffee and wait up for the reports. But you had better go now. It will be six o'clock before you get out of the building. Any later and there will be too many people about."

So here we were, running up the coast and running away from the world's troubles, if we could, for one bright day. I went below and woke Pat.

The sudden quietness as the motor died aroused me with a start. I sat up and looked through the porthole to see trees and rocks gliding slowly by. I recognized the little patch of brown sand set between two large green lichen-covered boulders. The anchor went down. We were at our island.

There were still two or three hours until sunset. The air was warm and the water calm in the sheltered cove. I yawned my way up on deck to see Pat, in a low cut bathing suit, spreading a large blanket for a sunbath.

We sat down on the blanket and she leaned over to pass me a cigarette. I took it, being careful not to look directly at her. There was much too much to see and my blood pressure was already high enough.

We smoked in silence for a while, watching the seagulls preen themselves on the rocks to which they had returned when the boat stopped moving.

"John, do you really believe the virus is a natural mutation?"

"I don't know, Baby, I just don't know."

"Then why do you keep arguing with Dr. Hallam about it?"

"I'm not arguing, Baby. I'm trying to keep this thing within the bounds of reason. We haven't a single bit of evidence yet to prove it isn't a natural disease, so why go overboard?"

"The structure of the virus isn't normal."

"So far, that seems to be so, but that doesn't prove it's synthetic either."

"But what if it does cause permanent damage to the ovaries?"

"Then, Toots, this old continent of North America is in one hell of a fix."

"I can't imagine how I'd feel if I got a disease and knew I could never have children."

"There are plenty of people that way now."

"Not millions of them, and not me! I always wanted babies but my husband wanted to wait. He was too busy making money...and having a good time."

"A good time with whom?"

"That's the question that finally broke it up. It's just as well there were no children, I suppose." She leaned over towards me and put her hands on mine. "If I ever marry again, I want a man who wants children."

This time I looked straight at her and the hell with my blood pressure.

"I want your kids," I said, and pulled her down into my arms.

She broke loose after a while, though I could feel her quivering. It was always the same. I had never been able to break down that last little bit of resistance, that fear of being hurt again. Maybe I never would. I sighed resignedly and sat up.

"Might as well go fishing," I said and I went to layout the lines and hoist the mainsail.

The wall of fog had been moving towards us over the empty sea like a great, flat-topped Antarctic iceberg, shining whitely in the gold light of the Western sun. Beside me, the mainsail hung slackly from the mast, the edge flipping idly in a stray puff of wind. Slowly the white cliff approached, and as slowly changed to an amoeboid mass of vapor, tumbling lazily, sending out streamers that twisted and vanished as they reached too far from the cool mother mist. One, stronger than the rest, waved a filmy pseudopod over my head and, for an instant, the gold light whitened. Another came, and another, and then we were gone, into the soft wet coolness of the seaborne cloud. The light faded, both from the fog blanket and from the setting of the sun. I hauled in the fishing lines and stowed them. I lit the running lights. I was shivering as I secured the sail, checked the gear and went below.

In the little triangular cabin, tucked under the forepart of the sloop, Pat was busy. The hissing of the pressure lamp and the crackling of hamburgers on the stove made a pleasant, home-like sound. It was cozy and warm here, in contrast to the fog-chill above. The smell of onions and beef drifted back to where I stood and I sniffed hungrily. She'd be a good wife, I thought as I watched her, and a good mistress too. She was still wearing her bathing suit and, as I looked from her full brown thighs up over the curving hipline to the small breasts pushing against the thin bra, I felt the slow pounding pulse and deep excitement of desire. Quietly I came close behind her. She started as my cold hands touched her, the instant of realization passed, and then she came back hard against me and her eyes were on mine as she turned her lips for my kiss. For a moment only she stayed, then, with a backward shove of her body, she tried to push me away.

"Look, darling, this is all very nice, but the hamburgers are burning."

"Let them," I whispered, my hands roving a bit. "I'm burning too."

"That can wait." Her eyes seemed to promise me as she brushed at a stray brown curl with the back of her hand. The spatula, waving above her head, flashed in the flickering gaslight. I let her go.

"Why don't you fix us a drink? There's time before we eat."

"If I drink too much I won't want you or the hamburgers either," I complained, but I went to the cooler and pulled out the gin and vermouth. "Someday," I thought morosely, "someday, she must give in."

I put her drink in the shelf where she could reach it as she worked and squeezed between the bench seat and the folding table while I watched her toss a salad. As a medical technician she was good, and the same thoroughness and skill went into her cooking; into everything she did for that matter.

The drink was good and the salad sat before me in its green crispness. Pat was lifting the hamburgers off the fire and, as the cracking ceased, I felt a low, insistent, base rumble rise above the hissing of the lamp. The night was quiet, no foghorns because there were no ships near enough. We had drifted fairly close to the mainland, behind some small islands, off the usual channels. The auxiliary motor was still shut down and for a moment I wondered if the currents had carried us in towards the rocks; but the noise was not the splash of waves on shore, it was too steady. Now Pat was standing, frying pan and spatula in either hand, and her straight dark eyebrows down in a frown of concentration.

"Do you hear it too?"

She nodded.

"Keep the hamburgers warm, I'm going up to have a look."

She moved back to the stove as I climbed up into the cockpit.

In a rising breeze the mist was swirling and, from the east, as the fog patches thinned out, the lighter cloud showed where a full moon lay hidden. The noise was louder now and coming fast, a beat of engines rising above the splash of wavelets against the bow of the sloop. I couldn't see where the ship was. There was no foghorn; neither the doleful groaning of the deep sea ships nor the sharp cough of the coastal steamer, bouncing its sound waves off the island hills, told me where it lay.

"The stupid oaf," I muttered to myself. "What's he doing in this deserted channel, and why doesn't he signal?"

There was no time to wonder. I jumped to the stern and grasped the tiller while I pushed down firmly on the starter button. The engine was cold and coughed reluctantly in the foggy air. I was still prodding the starter and working the throttle when the fog bank broke apart.

Above, to the east, the mottled moon, pale grey and blue like a Danish cheese, had risen over the Coast Range. Across the waters of the channel ran a rippling bar of light, cutting in half the white-walled arena of fog as the late afternoon sun pierces the dust of a Mexican corrida. Charging out of the misty north, like a Miura bull from the gate, came a black, highprowed ship, moving fast through its phosphorescent bow wave. It came on, straight for us, and the sputtering motor still did not respond. I stood up and worked the tiller back and forth, trying to scull with the rudder and swing our bow to starboard.

"Pat, Pat, for God's sake get on deck! It's a collision!"

I was still yelling when the thick black mass rose over me and the bowsprit of the sloop splintered and buckled. The jolt threw me to my knees but I held the rudder hard over and we slid by, bumping and scraping along the port side of the vessel.

It was not a big ship, but bigger than a halibut boat. It seemed about the size and shape of those floating canneries I'd seen in Hokkaido when I'd worked with the Japanese National Police in 1952. I don't know whether that thought was first in my mind or whether it came later but I do know, in the middle of all the confusion I heard a command screamed out in Japanese, and the answering *"Hai"* barked back as only the Japs can say it. I thought I must have been mistaken when, a moment later, I saw the man. The moon was full on his face as he leaned out over the side, near the stern. For an instant we were quite close as I stood up, cursing the stupid so-and-so's who were ruining the beautiful woodwork of my boat. He was fair-haired, with a short brush cut. The eyes were deep set and shadowed too much to see the color. His face was broad, with high cheekbones, and the mouth wide and heavy under a short nose. I couldn't tell his height, but he looked strong and stocky.

His hands, gripping the rail, seemed powerful even in that light. As we passed, the moonlight caught them and was reflected in a dull red glow from some large stone, a ring I presumed, on the back of his left hand. He didn't move or speak and I lost sight of him a second later when the pitching of the yacht in the stern wash threw me again to the deck. By the time I recovered, the steamer was across the open space and plunging back into the fog. In the swirling mist of its passage the flag at the stern fluttered out straight. It looked like a red ball on a white field.

"The hamburgers! My God, the hamburgers are on fire!"

I turned around, still dazed, to see Pat unscramble herself in the cockpit and drop back into the galley. I left her to it while I checked the wreckage of the port side fittings. We weren't holed, thank Goodness, so we could run for home under our own power. I steered in close to the shore of one of the islands where the fog had lifted, and dropped anchor. Then I went below. Pat was at the stove again. A new batch of hamburgers was under way and only a stain on the floor showed what had happened to the first lot.

"Mix us a drink, a big drink," was all she said, then.

The hamburgers were gone and we sat over our coffee. I was drowsy from the warmth and the hot sweetness of the Drambuie felt good as I took it slowly. Pat was rolling hers around the liqueur glass and watching the oily liquid slide back to the bottom. A quiet woman ordinarily, she was extremely so this night.

"Why so quiet, darling?" I reached for her hand. She looked at me and said nothing.

"Is it that damned ferret again?"

She nodded.

"Don't let it worry you so much, sweet. It's only a hunch and I don't think he's right."

"What if he is right, what then?" She went on without waiting for an answer. "I want children, I don't want to be sterile."

"Well you aren't, or at least I don't suppose so. Probably you won't be.

She looked at me scornfully. "What chance have I of avoiding the flu when millions of others are getting it?"

"Oh Lord, you women! Can't you see there's absolutely no evidence for this silly fear of yours? Damn Hallam and his wild ideas! Why don't you forget it?"

"Because I think he's right, that's why. She stood up abruptly. "Let's go on deck."

I followed her out into the cockpit. We were still at anchor, intending to start back after a few hours sleep. The sloop was as quiet as a resting seabird in the black shadow of a rocky point. It was cold. In a few minutes Pat shivered and came close to me, her arms about my waist. The keen air had awakened me, and, as I caressed her, smoothing away the little pebbles of gooseflesh on her shoulders and back, her warm body against mine stirred again the desire I had felt before the collision. She must have known. Slowly her arms came up and around my neck. Her head, cushioned on my chest, lifted and her full lips brushed mine lightly. For a moment I hesitated. Through the thin suit she felt naked under my hands, trembling with cold and excitement.

"I can't take much more of this, Pat," I whispered. "Either you quit right now or you go down to bed."

Her eyes opened. She looked straight at me for a long moment.

"Will your bunk hold both of us?" she asked as her lips closed hard on mine.

CHAPTER FOUR

WE came back through the big glass doors hand in hand. The night watchman, making his last round, nodded and smiled at us as we wound up the stairs to the penthouse. We went through the showers together since nobody else was about. I scrubbed her back to get rid of the salt sea crystals and was rewarded with a warm, wet kiss. We reached the living room just as Dr. Hallam, freshly shaven and bright, came in for his breakfast.

"Welcome back, kids!" he boomed at us. "Did you have a good time?" He looked closely at Pat.

A slow flush deepened the color of her cheeks and he grinned elfishly. "I see you did. Well, let's have some breakfast. I have news for you and plenty of work, so eat heartily."

He pushed the toaster buttons and the bread dropped out of the cooler-keeper and lowered itself into the heating element. I set three cups and three glasses under the dispenser and dialed tomato juice and medium strong coffee. Pat cracked six eggs into three plates, added bacon and pushed them into the slots in the electronic oven. A minute later, with his mouth full of toast and egg, Hallam mumbled,

"After you left I waited for about two hours before Smith phoned. He had a preliminary report on the female ferrets. You'll be glad to hear this, both of you. He couldn't find a thing on any of them."

"Wonderful!" Pat breathed, and smiled at me radiantly.

"What about the pregnant one?" I said.

"There were only the usual changes in the ovaries associated with pregnancy. "Mind you," he went on, "even with the new techniques, frozen sections are far from perfect, but I must admit I'd be disappointed if I weren't so relieved."

"Did the male ferrets show anything?" I said.

"He wasn't sure. He thought there were some inflammatory changes in the testicles but he wanted to wait for the paraffin sections to confirm it."

"Was there anything else?" Pat asked.

"Nothing except bronchial irritation, which one would expect."

It was eight o'clock when the telephone rang and I picked it up.

"Dr. Macdonald here," I said.

"Mac, is the boss in?" Smith asked.

"He's busy right now. Can I take a message?"

"Yes. Tell him the H and E's on those ferrets show only mild ovarian inflammation. The testicles are definitely inflamed…a low grade thing with a lot of lymphocytes. There is swelling and some degeneration of the sperm cells but it doesn't seem to affect the hormone secreting elements."

"What about other organs?"

"Aside from nasal and bronchial inflammation, essentially negative."

"Have you any suggestions?"

"It's too early to come to any conclusions but I'd like to follow up on this. How about taking biopsies on the male ferrets rather than sacrificing them. Then maybe we can see what is happening, I mean what the progression of the disease is, in the same animal. You could snip out a piece of ovary on some females too!"

"It isn't easy but we can do it."

"How about the other animals?"

"Some of the mice look a bit sick this morning, but the monkeys are still healthy."

"Well, if you can get the biopsies to us soon, we should have a good idea, late tonight or tomorrow morning, of what's going on. Say, I just had a thought! Didn't George inoculate some ferrets when the epidemic first broke out?"

"I wasn't here but I believe he did. Why don't you ask Harry? He was working with the Chief when I was away. All those animals are in the other section anyway."

"I'll do that. With yours in the acute stage and the others convalescent, we should get a good idea of the progress of the disease. I'll let you know later."

Hallam was in the ferret room. I joined him there and told him of Smith's suggestions.

"This is going to be quite a day," he grinned wryly.

He was so right. It took several hours, and innumerable bites and scratches from indignant animals, fortunately the plastic gloves were tough enough not to tear, before the last snarling male writhed back into his cage to lick his smarting personal property. We stopped for lunch and went back to the more complicated task of operating on the females in the afternoon.

In the meantime, the testicular biopsies, in their fluid-filled bottles, were on their way to Tissue Path., to join those that Smith and his residents were already preparing from the convalescent ferrets. Speaking into Dictape machines, the junior residents described and numbered the specimens while deft-fingered girl technicians wrapped them in little packets and put those in tiny perforated boxes. They dropped the boxes into beakers filled with fixative, which they then set up on the Technicon machines. The dials were set, the clock ticked, and hour by hour, as the timer clicked into the grooves of the wheel, the arms of the Technicon lifted, dangling their clusters of dripping boxes, turned like soldiers on parade, and dropped them again into the next beaker. On they went through the fixative that preserved the cells as they had been in life, the alcohols that slowly and carefully removed the water, the xylol that replaced the alcohol and, finally, the hardened, shreds of tissue lay in melted paraffin, ready for the cutting.

But first they had to be embedded in paper boats full of melted wax which, when it hardened, held them securely. Then, in millionths of a metre, the incredibly fine edge of the microtome sliced off a ribbon of tissue, as a bacon slicer cuts pork. The technician laid the ribbons on a bowl of warm water, separated off each individual slice with her needle and guided it on to a prepared glass slide, which was then laid aside to dry. That was not all. Now the process had to be reversed, the paraffin removed with xylol, the xylol with alcohol, the alcohol with water, before the pale white dots of tissue could be stained. There was no way of hurrying the process. Chemicals need time to react, and time they took, regardless of our impatience. At last the blue color of the Hematoxylin and the red of the eosin had been added in their turn and taken up by the tissues, the protective balsam and the slip cover had been placed over the sections; the slides had hardened enough to be put under the microscope.

With mounting excitement, Smith and his senior residents racked down the binocular microscopes to focus on the minute blue and red dots that lay beneath. Silently they looked, moving the slides jerkily but accurately with their fingers to view all the sections. Still silent, they swapped slides to check and recheck their findings. At last Smith straightened up and removed his spectacles. He rubbed his eyes wearily. He looked along the table at the three young men who had worked with him.

"Any doubts about this?" he said.

Three heads shook slightly. There was nothing to say. They were too tired for casual chatter. He pushed the Intercom switch.

"Dr. Hallam. Smith calling." The sound came into the living room as we sat at midnight coffee. The rasping voice jarred us out of the apathy of exhaustion.

"This is Hallam."

"George, we've just read those testicular biopsies. There's a subacute inflammation in those with the flu, as we saw before; in the convalescent ferrets there is complete absence of spermatozoa with no evidence of new formation."

I looked at Pat. "Now who should be worried?"

"I've never heard of this before in ferrets with the flu," Hallam was saying. "I'd think of mumps except that it isn't easily transmitted to the weasel tribe and this isn't like mumps clinically."

"What do you propose to do now?"

Hallam thought for a moment. "Carry on with our animal experiments; but we can't afford to wait for the monkeys. We shall have to start working on people."

"How?"

"Get in touch with the Public Health Department and see if you can round up volunteers for testicular biopsy in convalescents from the first attack. If they don't want a biopsy maybe you can persuade them to give us a sperm count."

"You know we can't keep this hushed up if we do that. The papers are bound to get hold of it."

"I realize that," Hallam said grimly, "but they're going to know sooner or later. Maybe this will soften the blow when it does come."

"OK George, you're the boss. We can't do anything until morning. I'm going to close up shop and let everybody get some sleep."

"Good idea. Keep away from the flu if you can."

"Huh, fat chance. I've got my family anyway. It's my kids I'm worried about."

"There are times when I'm glad I'm a bachelor," Hallam replied and shut off the speaker.

"Doesn't look too good, does it?" I said.

"We'll know by tomorrow night, I hope."

"I can't figure this thing at all. An inflammation that destroys the testicular cells should give a lot of swelling and pain. Those ferrets were frisky enough and they didn't show any signs of orchitis."

"Neither did most of the human victims," Hallam said.

"Perhaps it's only a temporary arrest in the maturation of the sperm rather than destruction of the spermatogonia themselves. That could be the explanation for the low grade inflammation and the minimal symptoms."

"You mean there might be some interference with an enzyme system?" Pat said.

"Yes. We see it in anemias where the cells don't mature properly because of a lack of some vitamin like B12. The same sort of thing could be happening here, I suppose."

"Then it might be only temporary?"

"I sincerely hope so, especially if Smith finds the same in man as he reports in the ferrets."

"I wish I could share your optimism John," the Director said, "but if this is a weapon it won't have just a temporary effect.   There would be no point to that."   He yawned. "Sufficient unto the day is the evil thereof, as the Good Book says. Let's go to bed."

The alarm jarred me out of deep sleep. As I groped beside the bed for the still vibrating clock. I regretfully abandoned my dreams for the austere grey walls of my temporary room, and the dreary window view of a wet Vancouver dawn. The tide was out and the slimy green-spattered mud and rocks of the estuary looked like a surrealistic painting of a hangover. At the water's edge, a school of fishing boats angled in the mud, their tilted trolling masts reminding me of the broken antennae of some strange crayfish, stranded and dead on a fish market floor. And dead they were. No smoke came from their humpbacked little cabins; no fisherman climbed the slanted decks.

I wondered if the epidemic had silenced their motors, or was it just not the season for fishing. Were the lusty trollers and seiners worrying about their lost virility and gone home to test it out? The newspapers had been asked to play down their sterility stories, which had caused so much consternation yesterday, but even so it was common knowledge that those who had had involvement of the sex glands might be sterile.

I turned down the corridor to the kitchen and started the coffee dispenser. Pat was still asleep after a late night coaxing reluctant male and female ferrets into the same cage and to be friends instead of messily murdering each other.   Chivalry among ferrets is not highly regarded, even with females in season. We wanted to see if they could produce families, not to see which one was the stronger sex. Tranquilizers are fine for the purpose but it takes a neat balance to eliminate the fight and keep the desire. Hallam was not around. He was an early riser and could probably be found watching the monkeys if I cared to go there. They had shown no symptoms as yet. Probably the incubation period was about the same as in man, and if so there had not been time for the fever to start.

I moved on again to the shower, taking it cool to clear my fuzzy head. Now there was little to do but wait; wait for the ferrets to get amorous; wait for the chattering monkeys to fall ill; wait for more biopsies of the human volunteers out there beyond the virus-proof walls of our chosen prison. I thought of the previous day, the second after our brief excursion. After breakfast we had rechecked the animals while Pat had transferred cultures, brought our records up to date and then Hallam and I sat in the living room playing cribbage while we waited for Smith's reports.

As he had predicted, the newspapers soon heard of the new investigations and the noon headlines, shown over the TV, were large and frightening. "Are Flu Victims Sterile?" the *Daily Mail* screamed hysterically in three inch letters and went into a long discourse based only on a cautious statement, attributed to Dr. Smith, that some experimental animals, after the flu, showed a decrease in procreative powers. *The Sun* was more cautious but the tune was the same. An hour after the papers appeared Hallam ordered all telephone lines to the Laboratory shut down and a short dictated speech, intended to calm the hysteria, was played continuously over the trunks and repeated on both radio and TV.

The mayor came to the hospital, as mad as a clucking hen whose eggs have been disturbed, as indeed they had. She cooled off considerably after Hallam spoke to her on the inside telephone, and, in cooperation with the local director of the RCMP, the head of the Metropolitan School Board, the Medical Officer of Health and various other officials summoned to the spot, agreed to form a Public Safety Committee to take immediate action if the need arose. They too, after their meeting, could only sit and wait for Smith's report.

"Why didn't you go down and talk to them sir?" I said later.

"I don't want to get the flu."

I smiled condescendingly. "Oh? I didn't think it would mean that much to you."

"It doesn't," he said levelly, "but it would to you and Pat if I brought it back up here with me."

There was nothing I could say. I have seldom felt so foolish.

Later in the day, I played a lazy game of cribbage with Hallam while Pat knitted and watched TV at the other end of the room. Deciding to have some fun, as the Chief dealt a new hand, I picked up the paper that was lying on the table.

"Say, Pat, here's a little item that should interest you," I said, and pretended to read. "Lovely woman scientist, possible Nobel prize winner, knits little things and dreams of rose-covered cottage. I always wanted at least ten children, our reporter quotes Mrs. —" I started loudly, cocking one eye over the top of the paper; but I didn't finish.

Pat got up abruptly. For an instant I thought she would throw the wool at me, needles and all.

"You stinker…you absolute stinker," she spat at me, and almost ran from the room.

"Lord! She must be getting stir crazy," I said, bewildered.

"John, sometimes I think you spent too many years overseas," Hallam said quietly. "You still can't imagine how a woman thinks."

That broke up the crib game. Neither of us had the heart to continue. For the first time I really began to imagine a world full of sterile people; the falling population; the frustrated family life; the emptying houses; the already empty schools.

"God, what a dreary prospect," I said aloud. "And we were worrying about overpopulation."

The Chief caught my train of thought but he just nodded. There was no answer.

An hour later the phone rang. He answered it and then turned to me with a smile. "That was a report from Smith about the ovaries of those convalescent ferrets I inoculated with the first cases of flu. They seem OK. Maybe it affects only a few females after all."

"Well, we can't go peeking into the tummies of all the ladies in Vancouver just to find out," I said.

"No, but we could try to get permission to biopsy ovaries on women who have abdominal operations in the city hospitals. Many of them have had the flu. It should tell us something."

He turned back to the telephone and in a matter of minutes Bruce Thompson had agreed to cooperate and to pass the word on to the surgical departments of the other hospitals in town.

Pat showed up to make us afternoon tea but she was clearly disturbed...even more so when she heard the news.

"I thought you'd have been pleased to hear about the females," I said dubiously.

"Suppose it does apply to women. What good are active ovaries to a prospective mother if all the men are sterile?" she said, scornfully.

"Well, you could always marry a Russian, when they take over the world."

"Fool," she sneered. "That probably will be years from now, and I'll be too old. For another thing, I don't want to be part of anybody's harem, even for a baby."

"Where do you get that harem stuff?" I grunted. "The Russkis aren't Moslems."

"This isn't your good day, John," Hallam interrupted. "It is obvious that there will be a tremendous demand for fertile males, and I can even visualize the female voters of this country and the United States demanding a quota for Russian immigrants to this continent. Just how the disgruntled American males would react I don't know. It could lead to a very nasty situation, and maybe to that retaliatory war the Reds are trying to avoid. Of course, it could also mean civil war...a war between the sexes with our males trying to revenge themselves on the Russians and our more realistic females trying to prevent it so they could use the Slavs to rebuild the nation...on Communist terms of course."

"Boy, this is really science fiction gone wild," I said. "Seems as if I picked the wrong place to live, unless I can avoid the flu."

Pat didn't even look at me after that crack. The day dragged on. Radio reports came every few minutes and the interruptions of the TV programs to announce the spread of the epidemics were almost as frequent as the commercials.

By now the Chinese had admitted that thousands were dying in the big cities of Peiping and Shanghai, while panic had disrupted communications to the interior. The first frightened reports were in from India, where efforts to block the Himalayan passes were too late and refugees had spread the deadly "measlepox", as it was now called, to Assam and Upper Bengal. There were rumors of flu in Texas and the Rangers had redoubled their efforts to keep the Mexican "wetbacks" from sneaking across the Rio Grande. All trans-Pacific air travel was cancelled.

About that time, the Intercom lit up again.

"Are you there, George?" It was Dr. Smith.

"Yes. What have you found?"

"We have the reports on thirty sperm counts taken today from professional personnel in this hospital. They are all negative."

"You mean normal. I hope."

"I mean negative for sperm. Three are from doctors who are just over the fever. They show a few abnormal forms in the secretion but no live ones. All the others are several days convalescent and show nothing but epithelial cells, a few polymorphs and more lymphocytes."

"What about the biopsies?"

"We have half a dozen that we rushed through. The slides aren't the best but it's perfectly obvious that something serious is happening. The spermatogonia are degenerating. The Sertoli cells seem all right and the interstitial cells are apparently untouched."

"What's he mean?" Pat whispered to me.

"He means the cells that form the sperm are dying but the ones that give a man his masculinity are intact."

53

"How many more biopsies have you?" said the Chief.

"About fifty."

"That's not enough. We're going to need at least several hundred. There must be absolutely no doubt in anyone's mind that this is a national emergency when we present the facts to the Government. I know that the statisticians can prove that this present number is highly significant but a politician is much more impressed with a lot of people than with a small group."

Joe Armstrong came on the line. "George, I'm convinced now that this virus does have serious after-effects. Let me talk to the other hospitals. We can get enough specimens in another twenty-four hours to prove your point." He paused, obviously considering his words. "I can't go along with this secret weapon idea yet...I don't think there's enough evidence. What do you say?"

"There isn't any evidence for the weapon theory," Hallam admitted, "but Gordon is well on the way to showing that the structure of the virus is synthetic. What I mean is that it looks more like a crazy mixture of mumps and flu than like any of the natural viruses or their known mutations."

"I still don't think we'd better let that story get out. There'll be enough hell raised as it is."

"All right...just as long as we stop this thing."

"How do you suggest we go about it?"

"Joe, there isn't time to search for a way of preventing it by vaccines. It will take months to manufacture enough, even if we succeed. Our only hope is to alert the civil authorities to its after-effects and get a strict quarantine set up. Frankly, I think it's almost hopeless by now. The Eastern Seaboard started reporting cases just a short time ago. Agents must be working in seaport cities like Montreal, New York, Charleston and all the others. I'm afraid we're licked except for isolated communities in the far north or in some rural areas, which can be ringed around with guards to prevent contamination. Every male we can save must be protected either until the disease dies out or we can devise a vaccine."

"Do you have any other ideas?"

"You could get a Blood Donor Program going to collect blood from those who have had the flu. We might be able to separate out antibodies from convalescent serum strong enough to give a temporary protection to those who haven't had the disease…and then hope for a vaccine."

"OK, George," said the Intercom. "Why don't you three stay in there and work on the vaccine since you haven't had the flu yet. I'll alert the Minister of Health. The Public Safety Committee is already back in session."

"Do that, Joe," Hallam said, "and tell Harry Cope and Polly Cripps to stay on call. We're going to need help with the electron pictures and other procedures."

So that day had gone by and here was another one, a day of coffee drinking and waiting, a day of writing reports, of listening to the mounting clamor in the outside world. In the Vancouver area, schools were closed at noon. The Public Safety Committee, impressed sufficiently by yesterday's preliminary reports, barred all public meetings and ordered theatres, bars and dance halls to close. Families not yet affected by the flu were urged to stock up on supplies and then remain home. Quarantine regulations were put in effect to protect them. This reversal of the usual procedure in which those who had not had the disease were kept isolated, was explained as necessary since the majority of the people had already been victims and therefore were unsalvageable. By nightfall the day's biopsy reports were coming in from all the city hospitals. There was no doubt. Every male who had had the flu was sterile!

The extras hit the streets an hour after dark. The Lieutenant Governor came on the TV and radio to declare a state of emergency. Curfew was to be enforced, beginning the next night, for all except essential medical services and food supply. At least the country was aroused. All trace of former unconcern had disappeared.

I went to bed early. There was nothing more I could do.

CHAPTER FIVE

AT midnight I awoke suddenly. My mind was alert and bright, with that extreme clarity which comes sometimes after working hard on a problem. The moon was pouring a pale light over the windowsill. It bathed my face in its lambent glow as I lay there for a moment, wondering what chemical time bomb had exploded in my brain. I looked at my watch. It was midnight.

I got up and looked out. Spreading up from the delta, curling over the fishing fleet and the canneries, flowing between the houses and filling the streets as the incoming tide runs in the channels and covers the stones of a rocky shore, the fog filled the hollows and smoothed over the humps of the city, until at last all but the higher tops of the buildings sank under the woolly wave.

The sense of urgent discovery had faded from my mind. There was something I had to remember, I knew, something that my mind had worked out as I slept, but, though I searched for a clue, it would not come. Idly, in my wakefulness, I watched the fishing fleet as it slowly sank in the mist, until at last even the tall masts were gone. A bad night to be out fishing, I thought, but a good night for smugglers or anybody who didn't want to be seen.

"By God...that's it! That must be it!"

The key had turned. The clue had been found. The sudden excitement of discovery set the pulse pounding in my ears until I thought it must be audible, like the ticking of an alarm clock. I opened the closet and rummaged in my suitcase for the sweater and light windbreaker and my old, cut-down paratrooper boots that I had brought from my apartment. It would be cold where I wanted to go, and go I must, virus or no virus.

I had just finished blousing my pants over my socks, GI style, and was moving towards the door when it opened, and Pat, holding a book in one hand, yawned in my face.

"What's all the noise about?" she said, standing there sleepily in her rumpled pajamas. The yawn froze in amazement and then snapped shut as her eyes traveled over me.

"Well, I declare!" she said. "Where on earth are you going?"

"I haven't time to explain," I said in a low voice, afraid of waking Hallam.

She suspected as much. "Have you told the Chief?"

"No. I don't want to tell him just now. I've got a hunch on this virus warfare idea of his. It's only a wild guess and I've got to go out to follow it up. He might not want me to take the risk of catching flu."

"I don't want you to either."

"I'm sorry, Honey, but I've got to do it. There's too much riding on this thing to let our personal affairs interfere."

"But you said yourself it's only a wild guess. Why risk our whole future on that?"

"Look, I'm going to keep away from people as much as possible, but I'm going out just the same. This may be the last chance I'll ever get to see if the boss is right."

"Then I'm going with you."

"Oh, hell! This is no job for a woman."

"It's no job for one man! Either I go or I wake up Dr. Hallam."

"All right," I said resignedly. "On your own head be it."

We trotted down the stairs and over to the parking lot. The Ferguson started easily and picked up speed quickly as the hydraulic drive fed power to the four wheels. I watched the center strip and wished for the radar control that was now being installed on the turnpikes south of the border. We didn't have it here yet so I had to rely on what little my eyes and ears revealed as we tunneled through the fog. Over the Burrard Bridge it seemed thinner and we made better time. We dived back into the depths along Georgia and I used the curb as a guide as we curved through Stanley Park and over the Lion's Gate bridge. The tunnel would have been quicker but I wanted to see the extent of the fog. At the center of the bridge it was too deep to tell but that in itself was encouraging. We swung around the cloverleaf and on to the old West Van road.

"Where are we going? Horseshoe Bay?" Pat said quietly, as she drew on a cigarette. It was the first time she had spoken since we started. I liked that about her; she could wait better than any other woman I knew.

"Yes, to the wharf."

"I'd like to know why, if you don't mind telling me."

"I don't mind at all. You should know," I said, and paused to reflect. "Light me a cigarette and I'll give you the whole picture as I see it."

I was lining up the facts in my mind as she put the burning cigarette to my lips.

"The first thing we have to do," I began, "is to assume that Hallam is right. If he is, if this is biological warfare, then how did it get started? There are several possible ways. The virus could be brought in by agents; it could be sprayed, or floated, or in some fashion sent ashore from ships or submarines; or it could be seeded from the air, either by aircraft or by something like those balloons the Japanese sent over on the air currents during World War II. Now, it started right in the city of Vancouver, so it seems to me that would rule out some of these possibilities.

"The balloon theory for one," Pat murmured.

"Right. Balloons drift as they please and anyway none has been reported. The same is true of airborne mists or floating devices. They would hardly have such a localized effect to begin with; that seems to rule out air or sea propagation, at least in the general sense."

"You mean except for agents coming by air or sea?"

"Exactly! Let's look at the air entry possibilities. The Russian air lines are now running regular over-the-pole flights that land here, but our customs people are quite strict and our mechanics help to service their planes. I doubt if they'd take a chance on bringing in stuff that way."

"What about freighters docking here or in New Westminster?"

"A very good possibility, but here too they have to evade customs and harbor police, and with the occasional seaman jumping ship to claim political asylum, the RCMP must keep a close watch on the movements of the crew. I think we have to rule this out."

"Then the only other way is agents coming overland; but that doesn't make sense," she objected. "Why would they come all the way out west, or if they sneaked in from Mexico, why start the epidemic up here in the north where we are so much stricter?"

"I don't believe these agents came by land, for the reasons you've mentioned. I believe they come in by sea."

"You mean by submarine?"

"No, although that would seem likely at first thought. There have been too many reports, in the last few years, of unidentified submarines off the coast. The Royal Canadian Navy and the United States Coastguard and Navy are watching all the time. It would be too big a risk." I stopped for emphasis. "You must remember Dr. Hallam's second postulate. The first was that this is a war. The second, that it is a hidden war. The presence of submarines along the coast would almost certainly cause suspicion…and that must not be, if the war is to succeed."

"Then I give up, John. How else could it be done?"

"By deep sea fishing boats."

"You mean Russian ships?"

"No, that would be obvious."

"Gracious, John, you are being obscure," she complained. "Then they must be communist Chinese."

"Wrong again! Still too obvious; and with the measlepox raising hell in China we wouldn't let any Chinese boat near the coast right now."

"For Goodness sake, stop being so mysterious. You sound like a murder mystery where the hero turns out to be the murderer."

"Not that either," I smiled and patted her silky knee.

She laid her head on my shoulder and sighed. "Sometimes, darling, I just give up on you. I'd be real annoyed if you weren't so sweet."

"All right, I'll tell you. It's Japanese fishing boats."

She lifted her head again to look at me in amazement. "Japanese! You mean the Japs are helping the Russians?"

"No, I mean the Russians are using Japs."

"Dear Lord," she murmured, "the man's gone nuts." She turned to face me. "And you were accusing the Chief of being fantastic."

"The whole thing is fantastic, but if we start by believing Dr. Hallam's assumption, incredible though it may seem, then we arrive, by elimination, at the solution I've just stated."

"You may have arrived," she said. "I haven't even started."

I butted my cigarette and threw it out. "Here's how it works," I said.

"We always think of the Russians as coming from Europe and of Russian agents approaching from the Atlantic side. That was largely the case until World War II, at least until the end of that war, when the Soviets moved out of Siberia and took over some of the old Japanese territory in Manchuria. Since then, as you probably know, they've really developed their naval bases on the North Pacific. Also, on the civilian side, they have developed a strong interest in the fisheries of the Aleutian area and they take part in the international agreements that control the salmon, halibut and other fishing in the North Pacific, as well as the fur seal trade. The result is that boats of all four nations, Soviet, Japanese, Canadian and American, plus some others, move freely about the waters of the North Pacific and along the shores of Alaska and British Columbia. As long as they abide by the Fisheries Commission regulations and stay out of territorial waters, they are free to move about pretty much as they please. That means that a fishing boat, or a floating cannery, could be out there right now, ostensibly looking for salmon, or tuna, or whatever is in season, and nobody would pay much attention to it among all the others. This coast is still wild and relatively unpopulated. I believe such a ship could creep in at night, close to shore, especially in a fog. The radar screens would have a hard time picking it out among these islands, especially if it had anti-radar devices. It would be a relatively easy matter to put a few men ashore from a fast motor boat almost anywhere around here."

"Where do the Japs come in?"

"That's the beauty of the whole idea. When I was in Hokkaido with the Japanese Defense Force, during the Korean War, I used to visit their defense positions in sight of the Kurile Islands and Sakhalin…the Japs called it Karafuto. The officers, many of whom had served in the Imperial Japanese Army, used to tell me about doing garrison duty there on Sakhalin before the Second World War, when the southern half was Japanese and the northern half Russian. They told me that many Japanese fishermen stayed behind when the islands were evacuated in 1945. What could be easier than to equip a ship and man it with an experienced communist Japanese crew?"

"You mean that ship that almost ran us down?"

"Yes, I do. That ship was flying the Japanese flag. The crew talked Japanese…but the man I saw looking over the stern at me was a Slav. Even if the ship got picked up they could claim Japanese origin and would be accused only of poaching on restricted fishing grounds, which happens all the time. Any Slavs aboard could pass as White Russians, residents of Japan, with forged papers."

"I remember that white man too," Pat said. "I got a glimpse of him just before the stern wash knocked me flat." She paused. "But surely you don't expect to go out and find that ship to-night?"

"No, I don't," I said thoughtfully. "The epidemic has been moving slowly inland and south. Dr. Hallam suggested that agents must have started it in the Interior of B.C., because of its explosive character. That makes sense, because they would want to get it started across the mountain barriers and the sparsely settled areas, so that the whole of North America would be affected: but they would still have to come back to the coast for supplies, and they probably arrange to do that when the satellite long range forecast says fog conditions are likely. Then, too, this is the last night before the curfew and they can still move freely. However, I'm afraid they are almost finished in this part of the world and will probably move on. I hope to see some evidence of them out at Horseshoe Bay. It's a wild chance," I concluded lamely, "like trying to throw boxcars in a crap game; but what else can I do?"

"What are boxcars?" she said.

"Double sixes…and an outside chance."

"It isn't even an outside chance," she argued. "Suppose you guess right and this is a good night for it, what makes you think out of all this long coastline they would pick Horseshoe Bay? I'd think a lonelier spot more likely. Why not between here and Squamish on the new highway, or farther south or north?"

"In the far north there are few roads. Closer to Vancouver the coast road has ferry crossings in it that would be time consuming and also, on a small ferry, strangers might be noticed more, coming and going. The same applies to the Vancouver-Squamish highway. A car parked along that road might attract attention and the little hamlets where they could land are too small for them to pass unnoticed. South of Horseshoe Bay are the busy shipping lanes and then the United States border country, so, to me, Horseshoe Bay seems the best bet. It's big enough that people come and go in their boats, even this late in the year, and don't attract too much attention. Cars are often left parked in the lots while the owners go fishing up the coast or visit their cottages for a weekend. Also, the floating docks for the small boats are beside the main jetty where we can see whoever passes, while we sit in our parked car. And there are a few lights, enough that we can see them without drawing attention to ourselves."

"You have it figured, don't you?" Pat yawned, but the yawn was more excitement than boredom.

"Yeah," I muttered, "but who knows how a communist thinks?"

It was about one-fifteen when we rode down the steep incline to the Bay and, after circling about the little beach park to look around, pulled in not far from the restaurant where the first dock light illuminated a small circle in the fog. We were far enough away under the trees to be safe, and, with the windows up, in that light, it isn't easy to see into a Ferguson anyway.

"Better not smoke," I said. "We can pretend we are here on a necking party."

"No pretense needed," Pat chuckled, and gave me a hug that nearly pulled off my right ear.

A heavy dig in the ribs jerked open my eyes and I came back out of my doze in a hurry.

"I hear somebody coming," Pat was whispering.

There had been a few late comers pass by, either to or from the dock, but all of them were obviously families, or couples, or fishermen. At any rate, nobody like our thickset friend had appeared in the hour past. Cuddling up to Pat's sweet-scented warmth, I'd fallen asleep in a matter of seconds. I could hear footsteps now, of several people, and shortly three men passed close by the car, going towards the water. One was tall and thin. He was wearing the heavy Squamish Indian sweater, made of unbleached wool, so popular with fishermen, a battered fedora and heavy work pants. As he passed he was speaking English with a slight European accent. The second man, of average height, wore an old dark windbreaker and slacks. His face, like that of the first man, was shaded by the hat he wore, a long peaked baseball cap. The third man was short but very strong looking. His head was bare, and, as they passed under the light, I saw a crop of close-cut, light-colored hair, and that unmistakable heavily boned face that had come so close to me out on the Straits. All three were carrying rucksacks over their shoulders. It was a clever disguise. They looked like campers, or perhaps transient workers, on the move from one lumber camp to another. Even their accents would be no hindrance with the country full of D.P.'s since the war.

"That's the man, John, the short one." Pat was pulling feverishly at my sleeve. "It's the same guy, I'm positive."

My heart was settling down after its first great leap, but my throat still felt like the ostrich that swallowed the grapefruit. They had gone on past the shore lamp now, and were almost lost in the darkness and fog of the main pier. I opened the door quietly and stepped out.

Pat grabbed at me. "John, don't be crazy! You can't handle three men alone."

"I don't intend to," I whispered, "but I've got to stop them somehow. We may never get another chance. They must be about through around here."

I broke loose and moved down the gravel road on to the wooden platform. I hadn't the faintest idea of what I was going to do. There wouldn't be time to call the police, and, even if I did, it might not do much good. Nobody outside of the Civic Hospital knew about the biological warfare theory. If I got involved in an argument I might end up in the police station, probably get the flu, and not be able to prove a thing. No, I'd have to handle this myself, play it strictly by ear and wait for the breaks.

The men were busy now over the canvas cover and mooring ropes of a fast-looking pleasure cruiser tied alongside the big jetty, with its bow to the open sea. There were hundreds like it on these waters and it would attract little attention. The short man was directing operations from the dock and his speech was perfect, colloquial American, from somewhere in the Northern United States or Canada.

"This one is probably the leader," I thought. "With an accent like that he could cross the border and never be noticed as he moved about the whole Pacific Northwest."

The fog seemed to be lifting in spots. It was getting lighter and a moon halo could be seen through the drifting clouds of mist. The three men were in a hurry. They didn't notice me until I was opposite their boat.

"I'd like to talk to you," I said to yellow-hair, who was bending over a bollard.

He started and straightened up quickly. I saw his head lift a little more as he got a good look at me.

"I'm busy; what do you want?" he grunted.

"I want something done about the damage to my boat," I said loudly.

The other two had stopped to watch me. At a nod from the leader, the second man went on getting the boat ready. The tall man stepped from the bow on to the main dock so he now stood a little behind yellow-hair and off towards the middle of the dock. I still had a clear line of retreat, but I didn't care for the setup; it isn't good tactics to be outflanked.

"I don't know what you are talking about." He had made the obvious answer.

"You know damn well," I said hotly. "You were on that Jap fishing boat that ran me down in the Straits of Georgia."

"You are mistaken. I know nothing about it." He turned away from me to get back to the mooring rope. I grabbed at his left arm. I think he was expecting it. He spun around with my pull, his right hand coming up and over, fast, for my head. I let go his arm and swayed to the right, hoping he wouldn't be too quick with a left hook. As his fist went by my neck I stepped across in front of him with my right foot, swung my backside hard into him and whipped downwards, using his right coat sleeve as a lever. His forward rush lifted him and he went over my back, high and fast, in the Judo version of the flying mare. I heard the gasp and the thud as his breath was driven out of him by the fall. Still crouching, I spun around, and, as I had hoped, the Russian beanpole was coming for me, hands out to shove me over the edge. It was simple. As he came in I fell back, gripping his arms, while my feet found his belly. He rocked over like a seesaw and I shoved up strongly with my legs to flip him. The Japs had clobbered me with that trick so often in the Judo classes that I had it down pat. This fellow really sailed. I heard his feet hit the water, but the splash was drowned out by the harsh aah of his scream when the small of his back smashed down on the edge of the dock.

"One down, two to go," I was thinking as I scrambled to my feet; but I had slowed down since the war. Too late, I saw that familiar thick shape above me, silhouetted against the clearing sky. In his upraised hand there was something round and black. Once again I glimpsed that dull red sparkle of the ring in the now bright moon.

"This proves it," I thought, so I lunged forward desperately, tackling him at the knees. Then the side of my head split and I dropped.

Dimly I heard a high-pitched screaming. I wasn't out cold; I could see but I couldn't seem to get up enough steam to move.

"That damn Russian surely is noisy," I thought dully. I looked up from my knees. Yellow-hair was on his feet again and he and the second man were scrabbling frantically over the side of the boat, dragging the tall man by the shoulders. I heard him groan, "Nyet, nyet!" as they tumbled him into the cockpit, limp as a pithed frog, and started the motor. I suppose the shock of the broken back had cut through the long indoctrination in the English language he must have had, for that was the first and last word of Russian I heard. The screaming kept up and then I realized it wasn't the injured man, but Pat, who had followed me down to the water. Being a really smart girl, she hadn't tried any heroics and had stayed too far from the fight to be caught, so, realizing that they couldn't dispose of the evidence, namely me, without a witness, the Russkis abandoned all pretense in a desperate scramble for safety in the fog that still blocked the harbor entrance. The cruiser foamed away from the dock with a deep roar, rocking the boats down the line of buoys.

The moment they were safely away, Pat was down on the planks, running wildly towards me. As she came close, she stubbed her foot on that same black cylinder that had downed me, and sent it rolling. She reached down and began tugging at my arms to lift me.

"Wait! Where's that thing? It may be evidence," I cried out, my head clearing fast.

"Oh come on! We must get out of here. Quick!" Pat was pulling at me as she spoke. "We can't afford to stay here and explain this to the police. They'd hold us for questioning and we mustn't risk any more exposure to the virus."

"The hell with the virus," I moaned as I stumbled along the deck, looking for the black cylinder. "Get the car started. I'm coming."

She turned and ran and, a moment later, with the cylinder in my pocket, I followed her. The Ferguson was already roaring as I jumped in beside Pat. She stamped on the accelerator and we went out of there and up the hill in a tire-ripping start that almost broke my neck. The engine has never been the same since.

The ride back was a painful haze. Every bump accentuated the throbbing in my head. Pat, grimly intent on getting well away from the area, held the pedal down as hard as she dared and the Ferguson whipped around the curves, its independently driven wheels screeching and scraping against the asphalt like the claws of a frightened dog on a waxed floor. The fog was gone except for little patches drifting down the gullies or hanging in dead air pockets between the hills. We reached a more brightly-lit area and she slowed down. There was no pursuit.

We went back up the stairs of the Lab and into the showers. I felt safe again like a wounded rabbit diving into its burrow. She helped me strip and, kneeling beside me, held me in her arms as I sat under the spray. The soft fullness of her breasts and arms, dripping with the cool water, made a nest of peace and comfort. For a long minute I let go and retreated back to childhood and the contentment of a mother's arms.

"My poor darling," she crooned, and rocked me gently, her slender hands smoothing my hair and caressing my face.

Suddenly I struggled to my feet and, slopping water over the floor, lurched back into the anteroom.

"The cylinder! I forgot the cylinder," I groaned, and flung open the door of the supersonic cabinet. The warning buzzer stopped. I fumbled agitatedly in the pocket of my windbreaker and drew out the thing that had hit me. For the first time I really looked at it. It was like an old-fashioned army aerosol bomb with a trigger mechanism on one end. I slammed shut the cabinet; the buzzer and warning light went on again.

Pat stood beside me anxiously, dripping heedlessly on the floor rug. "What was it, darling?"

"This thing," I held it out to show her. "There might be virus in it and I put it in the supersonic cabinet, like a damn fool."

"What will that do to it?"

"I don't know for sure. Ultrasound kills some organisms. Maybe it will be all right. It wasn't in there long." My stomach began to churn and I leaned on her weakly. "Oh, my head," I moaned. "I feel sick."

She put her arm around me and led me back to the showers. I sat down again, dropping under the spray, until the nausea had passed. Then I raised my head. "We've got to get this aerosol bomb to the culture room and start making tests. Hand me the soap darling."

Silently she reached it to me. I soaped the cylinder carefully, trying to sterilize it at least in part; then, after washing myself, I rinsed it off thoroughly. A few minutes later, in clean whites, we entered the living room. I slumped into a chair, elbows on the dining table, my head in my hands. Quietly efficient, Pat handed me two aspirin and codeine tablets for my pain and dialed strong coffee into a cup. She put in cream and sugar and pushed it over to me.

Hallam came in, in his pajamas. A light sleeper, he must have been disturbed by my heavy-footed entrance. He looked at us and his eyes puckered as he tried to see clearly without his glasses.

"John's been hurt, sir, but not badly," Pat said swiftly. "He'll tell you all about it in a minute. Let him recover a bit."

Without a word the Chief went to his room and came back. He had added a gown and glasses to his pajamas. He walked over to me and I showed him the goose egg on my head. He checked it and then looked at my eyes. Satisfied, he said his first words.

"Were you knocked out?"

"No sir, just dizzy. I think I'll be all right soon."

"Well, you know what to do. Let me know if you need help."

"I will."

He took the coffee Pat handed him and sat down opposite me.

"The bomb, Pat," I said. "You'd better take it now and get some cultures going." I took it out of my pocket and handed it to her. She reached for it and I thought she had it and let go. She fumbled.

"Watch out!" I shouted in alarm, and grabbed for it.

Either I startled her and she triggered it or my own hand struck the release. It doesn't matter now. A thin white stream of gas hissed out of the end and hit me squarely in the mouth. Pat stood there, rigid, the cursed thing still in her hands, and slowly her lips began to quiver and a big tear formed in the corner of her right eye.

"John...Oh, God!...the virus!"

"I'm afraid it is," I said quietly. I felt let down, finished, the same way I had when I watched the wounded die in the Aid Station and I couldn't help. Only this time I was the patient. Oh, I wasn't going to die, or even be very sick, but no man likes to think that he can never have a son to follow him, and I knew, beyond doubt, that in another week I'd be completely sterile.

I'd never seen Pat cry before and it brought me out of my daze. I went to her and took her shoulders in my hands and there, right in front of the Chief I told her, "Darling, I can't kiss you now, but I want you to know I love you and this will make no difference at all. It wasn't your fault."

She couldn't speak. I looked at Hallam. He sat there staring at the bomb in her hands.

"I think I can guess what has happened," he said, "but how?"

Quickly Pat sketched the story while I washed my face as well as I could. She finished and he stared into space. A few seconds later he put his big hands on the table and hunched to his feet.

"We still have to analyze the contents of this thing to see what kind of virus is in it...if there is. We might as well get started on the preliminaries. No sense in isolating ourselves any more. It's likely we'll all get the disease now." He looked at Pat's tear-stained face and said kindly, "Why don't you two go home for a rest before the day staff gets here. I can handle the beginning of this job myself."

CHAPTER SIX

IT wasn't far to Pat's apartment. The APC's were working and the ache in my head had gone, replaced by a soreness over the actual bruise. I drove slowly, reluctant to part with her now, to lose the sense of closeness we shared. Elation over our night's work, mixed with sadness for the future, had combined to bring us together more than we had ever been before. She said nothing, but her nearness to me and the hand laid gently on my leg were evidence enough of her feelings. At the stoplights I glanced at her, trying to gauge her thoughts. Her gaze was fixed on some nebulous point beyond the windshield; her face was still, frozen in its expression, almost as if she were a wax model.

Burrard bridge went by and I turned to the left, down a side street. The car rolled to a stop in front of a large modern apartment building. I shut off the engine, got out, and opened the car door for her. We walked up the steps together. She reached in her bag for the key.

"Don't bother coming back to the lab today," I said, turning to go. "Hallam can take care of it this morning and I'll go back later this afternoon and give him a hand."

She looked up in surprise. "You're having breakfast with me." It was not a question but a statement of fact.

"You're too tired, baby," I protested, but feebly. I hated cooking for myself and she knew it.

"I am a little tired," she admitted as she opened the door, "but bacon and eggs will pep us up. I want to talk to you."

Pat's apartment, a bachelor suite on the fourth floor, consisted of a bed-sitting room partly divided by an ornamental screen, a kitchenette and bathroom. Off the sitting room area, a tiny balcony with French doors overlooked English Bay. I strolled over to see the view. The fog was still hanging in patches to the shoreline but above the cottony masses it was a beautiful day and the mountains across Howe Sound sparkled icy white and blue in the distance. I felt a lift looking at them. Pat had removed her raincoat and hat. Now she turned from putting them in the closet to look critically at me, hands on her hips.

"Go take a shower and change clothes while I'm cooking breakfast," she said. "You look scruffy after that judo exhibition. Besides, I want to kiss you and you need a shave and you're covered with virus."

I came back, more comfortable in a clean shirt and slacks I'd left there on a previous occasion. She was sitting at the small dining table, looking over the morning paper. As I watched her read, concentrating on the epidemic story, I examined that kissable mouth, the strong straight nose, the thoughtful eyes. She wasn't the most beautiful woman I'd known but she was loyal, intelligent and good, clear through. Somewhere deep inside, a small ache began and grew. I hadn't thought much about marriage as we had agreed to let our friendship ripen into something better, if it wanted to. Now, as I watched her there, waiting for breakfast with me, I knew I was tired of our present relationship. It wasn't enough that she was my friend and, on one recent occasion, my mistress. I wanted her for a wife.

I was wondering how a childless marriage would work out when she looked up.

"Breakfast's ready any time you are," she said softly.

I went to her and raised her up. Then, slowly, without passion, I kissed her full on the lips. Her eyes were wide open and once more I saw the tears coming.

"John, don't...not now!" she whispered and turned away to start rattling around with the plates and the eggs and bacon.

We sat near the window over our coffee and cigarettes, looking out at the blue sky and scudding white clouds. The wind had dissipated the water vapor so that no wisp of fog was left. The little waves in the bay tumbled and sparkled in the light and a small tug burst through them importantly, steaming along like a short fat woman heading for the bargain counter.

"It's so beautiful, so peaceful out there," Pat murmured. "I can't believe we're in the middle of the greatest war in history."

"Well, if the number of casualties is any indication, it makes even atomic warfare look mild by comparison."

We had heard the news as we ate. The situation in Asia was rapidly approaching the catastrophic. In fact it was probably beyond redemption already in China, since the normal news channels had collapsed. All India was in a state of panic with hordes of people fleeing in any direction that seemed to promise escape. Southeast Asia was in an uproar, with riots and revolutions as reports of the inexorable advance of the measlepox filtered down to the people. In Africa, Egypt was already in the grip of the fatal disease. It was, as Pat said, not at all surprising, since Soviet technicians and supplies had been the mainstay of the country ever since the United Arab Republic was formed. The great desert barriers of Soudan and French Africa were holding temporarily, but it was merely a question of time before some poor devil, his fevered brain seeking escape, blundered to the forests of the Congo or the Cameroons, to the high country of Ethiopia and Kenya, and set fire to the rest of the continent. Only South America and Australia were still normal, if one could call normal the state of total mobilization and preparedness that was being ordered in practically every land which had sea or air contacts with the rest of the world.

In North America there was no measlepox. All the major cities of the east were reporting hundreds of thousands of cases of flu and it was rapidly spreading to the southern and inland areas.

"They must have had agents on the East Coast too!" Pat said as she listened to the announcer enumerating the cities and the estimated numbers of sick.

"I imagine so…a lot of them," I said. "Some of the spread must be due to natural infection too. There wouldn't be enough agents, and they couldn't carry enough virus to do all this."

"How do you think they got started over there?" Pat said. "They don't have the handy excuse of a fishing fleet, do they?"

"No, they don't. I imagine they use submarines especially equipped with tanks full of virus solution, or perhaps crystals, which could be mixed and loaded into aerosol bombs as required."

"But you said submarines might make our government suspicious."

"I did, but that was when the epidemic first started out here. It has been going on for some time now, in the west, and if you'll remember the broadcast, there were cases reported in Detroit, Chicago and St. Louis about the same time as in the coastal cities of the east. People will naturally think it has spread overland by air travel or train and won't be too concerned with what shipping is out in the Atlantic. The Red Fleet has been maneuvering frequently off Newfoundland for the past six or seven years so it shouldn't cause too much comment."

"If only they knew what was really happening to them!"

"I imagine the U.S. and Canadian governments do have our reports by now but they'll have to watch how the news is released. If they're not careful there could be a panic, with people evacuating the cities and spreading the disease. It takes time to organize police and military units for quarantine guards."

"How bad is it likely to be?" she asked.

"That's hard to say. The 1918 flu killed twenty million people and attacked about fifty times that number. Since then, ordinary flu epidemics have been reported with up to fifty percent of the people involved. The Asian flu of 1957 affected up to seventy-five percent in some areas. But this stuff isn't pure flu and so there may be absolutely no immunity. Probably the only thing that will prevent people from getting it is not to be near someone else who has it. In the old days that was possible, but with the population we have now, and the rapid communication between towns, it is much easier to spread an epidemic than it was fifty years ago. My guess is that eighty or ninety percent of the population will get it."

"John," Pat said thoughtfully, "How long is it likely to be before you start having symptoms?"

"You mean all of us, don't you?" I said. "After all, that spray must have splashed a bit and both you and the Chief may have got enough to infect you."

"Well, yes, if you put it that way."

"Oh, about four days," I guessed, "or, perhaps a day more or less. We aren't quite sure of the incubation period yet, and there's always a chance of a mutation with a shorter period if a synthetic virus is liable. We don't know that either."

"It's practically certain you'll be sterile, isn't it?

"I'm afraid so," I said ruefully.

"What about convalescent serum, wouldn't it help?" she asked hopefully.

"If I got a big enough and strong enough dose, it might. There isn't any ready yet. I asked Hallam just before we left this morning. If it isn't injected early it may modify the disease but probably wouldn't prevent it completely. I might still be sterile. It doesn't always work anyway."

"What about me?"

"Last night, before I went to bed, Dr. Hallam got a report that very few women had shown symptoms of sex gland involvement. The biopsies taken by Bruce Thompson from the ovaries of women who have had the flu showed only minor changes that Smith could detect. That isn't absolute proof that everything is all right, of course. It will take time to find that out."

"What about miscarriages in infected women," she persisted.

"They checked that out too. There have been occasional cases, but no more than you are likely to see with any heavy fever. That ferret may have been an exception. Perhaps it's a peculiarity of the ferret's reaction to the virus. It may prove to be a rare complication in people. Of course we don't know yet if the children of infected mothers will be born deformed in any way, as they often are in German measles. This virus may have no such power."

"Well, that's a chance I'll have to take," she said.

"What do you mean?" I queried. "You'll likely have the flu by next week and you don't even know if you're pregnant yet. You couldn't possibly tell so soon."

"I know that—and that's the reason I wanted to talk to you. "You and I have been letting things ride along for some time now. I've enjoyed it and I have no regrets. But it's time to stop; to make up our minds." She looked straight at me. "Do you love me enough to marry me?"

I got up and went to her. I put my arms around her and this time my kiss was not quiet.

"Silly question," I whispered against her cheek. "I was getting tired of being just the boyfriend. We'll go and get the license right now. We can get married as soon as the three day waiting period is over."

She looked up at me and said, "You wait here. I'll be ready in a minute."

I sat down and lit another cigarette. Three puffs later I heard her speak behind me.

"I'm ready, John."

I looked around and came to my feet with a gasp. Then I took her into my arms.

"Pat...my Pat! God, but you're lovely!" I smoothed back her hair and tilted her face to see her. "Darling, why are you doing this?"

"This is our wedding day, John. If we wait for a legal marriage it will be too late...you'll probably have the flu. I slept with you on the boat because I wanted your child and I was afraid of the flu. Now I'm sure you'll get it. This is our last chance." She moved away from me and took my hand.

Later, as we lay quietly together, I said teasingly, "What's it going to be? Boy or girl?"

"I really don't care. I only hope he'll have a few playmates to keep him company. An only child in a family is bad enough. I don't want him to be lonely."

I pulled her over to me and held her tightly. Her tears were warm against my neck.

CHAPTER SEVEN

TIRED, rumpled, but elated, Dr. Hallam met us as we came out of the dressing rooms the next morning.

"My theory was right. The bomb was full of virus," he said, his face lighting up happily for an instant. Then, as the thrill of discovery faded, grimness clouded his eyes. "At least now I can prove what we are up against, thanks to you two."

Clinging to my arm, Pat looked at me and sighed, "Thanks to John! But the cost was high."

"Maybe that price won't have to be paid. They've been working all night in Serology, since I determined that the virus gave the same reactions as the flu virus, to concentrate immune globulins from convalescent sera. They just sent up a hundred c.c.'s." He indicated a packet on the table.

"John can take the first dose right now."

"That's fine," I said, "and I certainly appreciate it, but why should I get the serum when other doctors on the outside, treating flu patients all day long, are not getting it. That's hardly fair."

"Democratically speaking, it should be distributed by lot," Hallam said, "but there's no time to argue the point. If it will ease your conscience any, you're getting it, not because of favoritism, but because you, and Pat and I too, are the subjects of the first controlled experiment on human beings with the new virus. We know exactly when we were exposed to it; we know that you, at least, received a very heavily concentrated dose, and if this globulin proves effective then we can start issuing it in large quantities. The word has already gone out through the Public Health Service, to collect blood and process the serum. By the time we find out if it protects us, it will be in bottles ready for issue all over the country. It's a terribly expensive and cumbersome way compared to using a vaccine, but we have no alternative. They haven't yet got an antibiotic that will attack the flu virus. But we're wasting time! C'mon, drop those pants and take your medicine."

Later, as we sat gingerly on the hard chairs around the dining table, Hallam outlined his plans.

"We won't work with antisera at all. The Routine Lab can handle that. What I want to do up here is to produce something that will give active, permanent immunity...not just passive immunity that has to be repeated every week."

"You mean to produce a vaccine?" Pat asked.

"That's one way. We could try killed virus, formalin treated, something like the method Salk used for the polio vaccine. But that too can be done in the Public Health Labs or by the big drug companies. They have all the equipment set up for it."

"It takes at least three months from isolation of virus to production of vaccine...and another three or more until everybody can get a shot."

"Righto, John. It must be done of course, but I'm going to tackle the problem in another way. Maybe we can shorten the time."

"How will you do it?"

Hallam turned to Pat. "I don't say we can do it. We shall try. If we could alter the virus enough, by physical or chemical treatment, to knock out only the sterility effect, we could let people have the flu. Then it would be necessary only to produce a limited amount of the new virus and start it going all over the country."

"That would eliminate all the processing of killed virus, sterilization and so on," Pat said excitedly.

"And everybody who had the virus would produce more and spread it, faster than the drug companies could make it," I added.

"Precisely...if it works," Hallam said. "That's what we will concentrate on. Biochem is analyzing the structure of the virus. They are going to advise us when they get the nucleoproteins sorted out. We may be lucky. Sometimes substituting a methyl group by hydrogen or changing the positions slightly will make a tremendous difference in properties of the molecules. It will have to be rather a hit and miss program. There isn't time to work out the full formula of the virus. By the way, have you seen the paper this morning?"

"Not yet," Pat said.

"They have a new name for it now—Sterility Flu, or S-Flu for short."

"Yeah, short for flu but long for sterility," I muttered.

"Maybe the sperm cells will regenerate after a few months," Pat said hopefully.

"I wouldn't put any down payments on a baby carriage if I were you," I said, as we moved towards the workrooms.

It was the third morning after the fight on the docks. Pat had finished injecting an enormous dose of concentrated human serum into my left buttock and was giggling at my choice selection of swear words when the phone rang. I answered struggling with my pants at the same time.

"Cope here," it said. "Is that you, John?"

"Yes Harry, how are you?"

"I'm afraid I've caught the flu, laddie." He was obviously trying to sound unconcerned. "'I've got a fever and all the aches and pains that go with the ruddy stuff. I wanted to tell the Old Man I shan't be working for a day or two."

"Damn it, that's a shame," I said. "Look Harry, why don't you come up here and let us give you some serum, it might forestall the complications."

"Might as well, I suppose, but isn't it too late, really?"

"Too late for the flu, of course, but maybe not too late for the orchitis."

"Right-o," he sounded resigned. "I'll see you in half an hour."

"Wait!" I had the receiver halfway down before I remembered. "Better bring Polly along too. If she hasn't got the flu now, she probably will have."

"Will do," he answered and cut me off.

Pat heard us talking but Hallam was away and would have to be told later. Nowadays he was seldom available, being constantly in conference or on the telephone talking to specialists in preventive medicine or virology from other parts of the Americas or Europe. For the moment, Vancouver was the center of attention of the western world. Most of the NATO countries by now were battling full scale epidemics of their own and wanted to know what we had found out about the disease.

All over the province the schools, theaters and all public meeting places had been closed. All main routes of travel were under police and military control and only the most essential transport was allowed on the highways, the rails, or in the air. The same precautions were soon put into effect across Canada. The United States was under martial law, with the National Guard in complete control in each state. Communities that had not yet reported cases of S-Flu were isolated for their own protection and supplies were sent to them by military convoy. The guards and truck drivers were men who had already had the disease and were no longer infectious as far as anyone could tell. Even so, they were not allowed to come close to the isolated ones who unloaded the supplies with the greatest care after the truck drivers had got out and moved away. In spite of the most stringent precautions, the disease still broke through into some of those areas, and, as the weeks passed by, the uninfected zones were reduced to such locations as small hamlets in the eastern and western mountains, little whistle stops on the prairies and, in the southwest, some of the desert communities.

When the truth about the S-Flu became known, many families in the cities tried to barricade themselves in their homes. Some had already been exposed to the virus and hunger drove others out, only to catch the disease. Later, when the public health services were better organized, the same isolation techniques used on whole villages were used wherever a family was found untouched. Even in the worst areas a few were known. There were, of course, the cranks and selfish ones who couldn't bear to see others escape their own fate, but as a rule the people responded well. They knew, finally, it was either that or race suicide.

Ten days after exposure the three of us were in fine condition, although my behind felt as if a porcupine had attacked me, from all the injections of serum.

As I complained to Pat, "You women are lucky. You have a bigger target for all these damn needles."

Two weeks went by without a sign of S-Flu and, once more, when it seemed definite that we had escaped, we were locked up again in the Lab. Under the military orders covering all uninfected persons, we had to be isolated, but, as we were still working with the virus, the Research Building was the obvious place. To me, there was only one thing really wrong with the situation. In all the rush and excitement of our research, we had not yet taken out our marriage license, so, not being completely brazen, we had to take to our separate rooms and beds again, with the Chief as chaperone to our physically consummated but legally unlawful union.

I said to Pat when we were locked up, "That does it! Now, if you really are pregnant, all the women will condemn you as a fallen sister while envying you for being with child...besides wondering whose child."

She chuckled. "A most unusual situation, and one I intend to exploit to the fullest extent."

"Do you think you are pregnant?" I said hopefully. "You ought to be, I'm plum wore out trying."

"Well, I'm not ready to take up knitting yet," she joked, "but there are encouraging signs."

All across the continent, virus laboratories were working continuously and almost exclusively with the S-Flu. A number of experiments using convalescent serum were in progress but, as it was not known exactly who had been exposed to virus, and when, the results were hard to evaluate. Now we had proof. We three had been exposed to virus at a known time and yet, two weeks later, there we were as healthy as ever. When the news was published, every blood bank in the country was swamped with volunteers. At first the convalescent serum was given only to the males...a dramatic reversal of the laws of chivalry...but the women did not complain. They knew that without fertile men there could be no children and to most of them such a world seemed empty indeed. Gradually, as supplies increased, all non-infected persons living in contaminated areas received weekly doses which, though much less than I had had, were found to give sufficient protection in most cases. It was still not known if there were any ill effects on unborn children so pregnant women were also included in the schedule. Where injections were given, and no new cases reported, the quarantine was lifted after a while, but where the disease had never reached, the population was still isolated, awaiting the day when a permanent vaccine would be available. Sporadic outbreaks of the disease were still to occur, months and even years later, among those who had never had it, but at last the major epidemic was over. The discovery, at the Medical Center of New York, of a protective vaccine, eventually made isolation unnecessary.

Long before that happened, the restriction on our movements was lifted. Only those in the uncontaminated areas were confined to their own locality. The rest of us, provided we took our weekly serum shots, were let loose.

"Now I can make an honest woman out of you," I joked as we walked out of the Lab and breathed gratefully the cool damp air of early winter.

"You don't need to darling," Pat said. "If I am pregnant there's at least a million women envying me right now. When it was easy to get pregnant it was proper to do it only in holy wedlock, as they say, but moral standards are changing already. To be pregnant is an honor, illegitimately or otherwise. I imagine before long there will be a lot of husbands looking the other way or condoning artificial insemination if they can have sons thereby."

"You still want to get married, don't you?"

"Of course, sweetheart," she squeezed my arm, "but I want a proper wedding, not a civil ceremony, and we haven't time for it now."

Late one afternoon shortly before Christmas we were sitting contentedly in front of the fire in Pat's apartment when the front door buzzer sounded. She pressed the speaker button.

"Hello, who's there?"

"It's Hallam. I've brought you a visitor. May we come up?"

"Certainly, come right in."

A few moments later they walked through the opened door.

"This is Inspector James of the RCMP," said Hallam, introducing a tall, thin, grey-haired man in civilian clothes.

"Won't you sit down?" Pat indicated chairs by the fire.

"How about a drink?" I said to the Inspector.

"If you're having one."

"We were going to. Dr. Hallam likes Scotch and water. With a name like yours you might like the same."

"That will be fine, thank you."

I brought their drinks and poured our usual gin and Italian vermouth for Pat and myself.

"Inspector James has been in charge of the investigation into the virus warfare theory," Dr. Hallam began. "He knows your stories already but something new has come up and he wanted to talk to you." He settled back in his chair and looked over at James.

Inspector James took his cue. "Since Dr. Hallam proved that the aerosol bomb contained virus, we have been trying to track down all possible agents, and our maritime division has been searching for the ship off our coast. We have been in constant contact with the FBI and the US Coastguard, and through them, with the US Armed Forces. As far as we can determine, one group of saboteurs inoculated the Vancouver area, the Interior of British Columbia and the Pacific Northwest. Then they disappeared."

"You actually traced some of them?" Pat asked.

"No, I'm afraid we didn't," James said ruefully. "We base our conclusions on indirect evidence, stories like those Dr. Macdonald found in the public health reports, you know, aerosol bombs triggered off accidentally and so on. The epidemic pattern in BC is now following a more natural course so we believe the agents left...probably they were recalled right after that fight you had."

"There might still be some undercover agents left," I guessed. "Natural epidemics tend to die out, even as virulent as this one is. However, if they give it a boost from time to time, they might get eighty or ninety percent of the population. Anything less wouldn't be too damaging, we could make up the population deficit in a few years."

"We thought of that, Doctor, and we are continuing the search. However, the main party of agents appears to have left.

Some days after your fight, routine air patrols noticed what could have been the Japanese fishing boat off California. Not long afterwards, San Francisco, Los Angeles and San Diego had their first outbreaks. Unfortunately our governments had not yet given the order to find and arrest all agents. By the time that order was given, the ship had disappeared. We presume it stayed out at sea. The epidemics in Mexico originated in Monterey, Vera Cruz and Mexico City, which makes us think they were started by saboteurs operating from the Atlantic side."

"Last week there was the beginning of an epidemic in Medellin, Colombia, and then in Guayaquil, Ecuador, which appeared separately from the already established disease in Rio de Janeiro, Buenos Aires and other eastern cities of South America. Our consulates and the United States embassies in those countries had been warned and passed the word on to our Latin American friends." He paused to drink his Scotch and then continued. "The countries concerned have been searching their coasts for any sign of strange vessels but without success until yesterday."

"You mean they found the boat?" I interrupted hopefully.

"I believe so," he said. "Ecuador, as you know, owns the Galapagos Islands, well off the coast, and for many years a favorite out-of-the-way retreat for all sorts of people. Now Ecuador claims fishing grounds a great distance off her coast and around the islands. This has led to a lot of international incidents and sometimes to confiscation of fishing boats stopped inside these limits by Ecuadorian gunboats and charged with poaching. Well, these annoying rules proved very useful yesterday. A spotter plane found a black cannery ship flying a Japanese flag in the waters off the Galapagos. That vessel is now anchored in the main harbor—I forget the name—under the guns of a patrol boat."

"Wonderful," Pat breathed. "What about the crew?"

"I haven't any information about them but I do have a request from the Department of State of the U.S.A. that you fly down to Ecuador and, with their consular officials, and I suppose the Ecuadorian authorities, go to the Galapagos to see the ship and crew. This is necessary because it must be kept secret. We don't want the Communists, if that's who they are, to get suspicious. This must look like a simple arrest for poaching, at least for the present."

"Do both of us go?" I said.

"That was the intention, since you both saw the men and the boat," the Inspector smiled, "and of course all expenses will be paid."

"Oh boy!" I looked at Pat. "Christmas this year is going to be a summer vacation…the one we didn't get."

We flew south to Quito in one of the fast new jets of the Canadian Pacific Airlines and from there to the Galapagos in a much less comfortable Ecuadorian Air Force transport plane. The airstrip on Baltra Island, so busy during World War II, lay neglected and forlorn among the lava blocks and scrub. From it to the Governor's house on Chatham Island, we rode first by motor launch and then in a rusty old jeep, probably another relic of that war or subsequent lend-lease.

"I wish I could see a tortoise," I said, clinging desperately to the struts of the canvas top as we bounded through clouds of dust from the jeep ahead.

"They're probably all in zoos now," Pat said, mopping cautiously at her face where the makeup was slowly melting in the steamy tropical heat. "You couldn't see one anyway in this dust."

It was a little cooler on the screened-in porch of the residence. The Governor, a fat little man who looked like the caricature of a Mexican snoozing under a tree, fussed around all the important visitors. With obvious pride he produced cold drinks from what was probably the only refrigerator on the island. I took a long draught of beer, settled back with a sigh and looked out over Wreck Bay.

"Hey! There's the fishing boat." I sat up again excitedly and pointed it out to Pat. The officials exchanged nods and smiles.

It was the boat...the first test of identification was over. An hour later we went aboard although there was nothing to see that could be of use in solving the case. All the tanks intended for holding fish were empty and had been flushed with seawater. One tank held fish when the ship was captured, probably as camouflage. There was a well-equipped laboratory but that had been explained away as necessary for marine biology research. There was absolutely no clue. No trace of aerosol bombs or other apparatus for holding the virus had been found.

Ashore again, we were taken to see the prisoners, watching them through peepholes as they exercised in the small jail yard. Almost at once Pat shook me and tried to point through the little peephole before she realized how silly that was.

"Did you see that tall man on crutches?"

"Yes, it's the one I tossed on the deck."

"And there's the second man, and...look over to the right there, by the wall! That's the leader, I'm sure of it!"

"Wait till he comes closer," I said, "but I think you're right."

The crewmembers were circling around the yard, getting exercise under supervision of the guards. As they came closer to our hiding place there was no doubt. Yellow-hair and his pals were there.

One by one, the three Slavs were called in to stand before us. The blond leader was first. I thought his eyes widened a little when he saw me. There must certainly have been despair in his heart when he realized that they were not being held as poachers, but his control was admirable.

"Do you know these people?" The question was in English.

"No."

"You never saw them before?"

"No."

"What about that night at Horseshoe Bay," I broke in.

"I don't know what you are talking about."

It was useless, and had been from the start. All three men stuck to the same story. They were White Russians in the pay of a Japanese fishing company, partly as laboratory workers and partly for their ability to speak several languages.

We went back to the Governor's house feeling defeated. This was an anticlimax. The only points in our favor were that we had recognized the boat and three crewmembers immediately, and our descriptions of the men, given in Canada, corresponded quite well with their present appearance. Unfortunately, I had washed the fingerprints off the aerosol bomb in the shower, and with them, the only material evidence of the Russians' connection with the S-Flu. Or was it? I was thinking over the problem as we sat down to a late lunch.

While we ate both the Ecuadorians and Americans questioned us politely but thoroughly. As they explained to us, the question of identity was extremely important. We were the only witnesses that the captured Russians had actually possessed a virus-filled aerosol bomb and on that one fact might rest the future of the world. Where they had come from was by no means certain. The ship's papers, and those of the crew indicated Hakodate as their port of origin but the Japanese embassy in Quito had indignantly repudiated them, insisting that no such ship was registered in Hokkaido. There was nothing to link them with the USSR, which had not bothered, so far, to answer the first discreet inquiries.

"Did the Russians tell you where they came from?" I asked.

"From Hokkaido," the American military attaché said.

"No, no, I mean recently. Where has the ship been sailing."

"They claim they've been following currents across the Pacific, looking for new fishing grounds."

"Then they were not near British Columbia?"

"Not according to their stories, nor to the ship's log."

"There's a couple of ways we might check that. The Russians went ashore in B.C. Maybe they'll have pollen grains or dust in their clothes that could be traced to that part of the world."

"It's a possibility. We'll look into it."

"And then there's my sloop. We scraped along the side of the fishing boat and some paint must have come off. I haven't had time to repair it. At least that might prove we have met before, if the paints are similar, which would make our bomb warfare theory much more credible."

"It certainly would. We need all the evidence we can get."

"What are you going to do with them?" I asked the senior American officer after lunch.

"We have practically convinced the Ecuadorians that these people are really saboteurs, but naturally nobody is going to say anything about that. Our Latin friends are past masters of the art of 'mañana'—I think they could give the Russians and Chinese lessons in procrastination. They have agreed to hold the ship as long as they can on the poaching charge. If neither the Japs nor the Soviets claim it, that could mean indefinitely. I think it's too late to do much good," he concluded thoughtfully. "The epidemic is already out of control down here. The health services are too small and the distances too great, to say nothing of the lack of education of many of the people, ever to stop a pandemic without outside help. We in the States used to send aid but this time we have our own hands full."

"It sounds pretty hopeless."

"It is. Thank God the measlepox isn't here too or this continent would go back to the jungle."

Back in Quito I stood with Pat on the balcony of our room. We were both quiet, pleasantly tired. In another few days we would have to return to the Northern Hemisphere and winter, but here, under the summer moon, it was almost impossible to imagine. I looked over the railing down the narrow street with its high-walled houses. In the cool air the faint sound of music and singing carried up from the town. Apparently the flu couldn't dampen all the liveliness of these people.

"If I had a guitar I'd get down there in the street and serenade you," I said playfully, my arm around her slim waist.

"If you could sing, I wouldn't mind," she retorted.

"Doggone it, already you sound more like a wife than a mistress," I complained. "Where have all those romantic ideas and that passionate lovemaking gone?"

She batted her eyes at me. "Why don't you take me inside and find out."

CHAPTER EIGHT

IN the early part of the new year, work piled up increasingly. Under instruction from the Minister of Health of British Columbia, the Virus Research Laboratory was turned over to federal control. In addition to our attempt to modify the S-Flu, we were engaged in highly secret research on the synthesis of viruses, in cooperation with the National Research Council of Canada and its American counterpart. Pat was still working although sometimes she was extremely tired and I was worried about her. The work was so secret that, instead of marrying me and settling down to being a housewife, she had stayed on at the Lab at the Chief's urgent request. She and Polly, besides being the best technicians in the hospital, were the only ones who knew the whole story of the virus war. Hallam knew by now that we were living together constantly but we all realized that there was no time for a honeymoon and the legal ceremony didn't seem very important under the circumstances.

A few weeks after our return from Quito the Chief had been called to Ottawa. On his return Pat invited him to our apartment for dinner. Polly and Harry made up the party. A couple of cocktails before dinner loosened our tongues and even Harry, who had been rather morose since the flu caught him, was able to laugh at the Chief's fund of good stories. Polly was her loquacious self again, I noted. Having the flu shortly after Harry hadn't bothered her much, but Harry's evident depression had.

After a heaping plate of lasagne and a large slice of fresh apple pie, Hallam sat back and loosened his belt with a sigh of repletion.

"It may be bad manners," he admitted with a smile, "but if I don't, I'll explode."

I offered him either a Drambuie or Australian port to go with his cigar. It was difficult choice as he loved both. The port won, for patriotic reasons, he said, and he tippled and puffed for a few minutes in complete contentment.

"You know, if I'd been ten years younger I'd have proposed to you myself." He winked at Pat. "The only trouble is that I wouldn't have been able to decide whether to keep you in the Lab or have you stay home to cook."

For a moment there was silence as we watched the fire. Then the Chief took a deep breath and let it whistle out of his nose.

"You're waiting to hear what happened down East, I imagine."

We all nodded and he continued. "When I arrived in Ottawa I checked with the Minister of Health but he wouldn't tell me anything. The following morning we flew to Washington where we were to attend a top secret conference headed by Prime Minister Macpherson of Canada and President Johnson of the United States." He paused. "Johnson, you remember, was the dark horse Democrat who swept the country after the moderate depression of the late fifties and the consequent decline in popularity of the Republicans."

"Anyway," he resumed, "the senior members of the Canadian cabinet and corresponding members of the United States Executive and Congress were to be there, as well as the military heads and observers from the British Commonwealth countries which had representation in Washington. The next morning, in the underground military headquarters, which had been prepared for thermonuclear warfare, we assembled at our appointed desks. With their usual love for conferences, the Americans had made elaborate preparations, and we all had name tags and name plates on our desks, as well as microphones and loudspeakers so we could identify and hear anyone in the room. With very little preamble, both heads of state were introduced. The President was the first to speak. I'll try to give it to you as he said it."

"Gentlemen," the President began, "for one hundred and fifty years our two governments have been at peace and for the greater part of that time we have cooperated amicably on major problems. Since World War Two, that cooperation has continued with such projects as the Saint Lawrence Seaway, the DEW line, the various military highways, coordination of defense plans and military maneuvers, so it seems natural that we should cooperate now, in what I honestly believe is the greatest threat we have ever faced. The Prime Minister and I have already talked this over and he agrees with me that because of the peculiar nature of this world war…and I have no doubt that it is war…we can make no public announcements at present, nor should we retaliate in ways which will cause greater harm to our people than they have already suffered." He paused briefly. "Let me make that concept clear.

"As most of you know by now, sterility flu is a synthetic disease agent introduced into the democratic nations by agents of the USSR. The evidence for this seems conclusive, especially as our own agents have succeeded in getting to us a few samples of the vaccines used to inoculate the school children and the members of the military services of that country. These vaccines were in use before…I emphasize…BEFORE sterility flu was reported in the western world. Our scientists tell me they contain protection against the S-Flu and probably, though this is not yet proved beyond doubt, against the so-called measlepox which is killing millions of people in Asia and Africa. We have indirect evidence that these same vaccines were also used to protect large numbers of Soviet civilians, adults that is, but not all of them. It has been extremely difficult and dangerous for our agents to obtain enough samples for testing as the vaccines are closely guarded and the whole manufacturing process is of the utmost secrecy. Apparently the dictatorial clique has decided to sacrifice a large number of unwanted human beings in the interests of Communism, under the guise of breeding a better race by elimination of undesirables. By sacrificing part of their own population they hope to persuade us that they, too, are innocent victims of worldwide pandemics. With this diabolical plot they hope to avoid the inevitable retaliation that would follow an open act of war such as a hydrogen bomb attack."

There was murmuring through the assembly. Many of the lawmakers had not known all the facts before the conference and none had seen the attack develop as we had.

"The credit for the discovery of this plot goes to Dr. Hallam of Vancouver, Canada, who is here in this room. He first suspected it and one of his associates, an American and former member of the United States Army Medical Corps, had the courage and good fortune to capture the first piece of vital evidence which proves this theory. It was an aerosol bomb, in the hands of men posing as recent immigrants to North America. By an extraordinary coincidence, and shrewd deduction, this gentleman was able to point to the ship that brought these men ashore. In fact his boat was in collision with the vessel as was subsequently proved by comparing paint scars and analyzing the chemical composition of the paint from the two vessels. This gave us enough evidence to put our agents in Russia to work, with the result I have mentioned. If it were not for Dr. Hallam's deductions about the nature of the disease, and the early use of anti-serum, we should today be in an almost hopeless situation.

"As a result of this bacteriological, or rather virus warfare, we estimate that at least eighty percent of the population of India, China, the East Indies and Africa has died or will die from measlepox. There is no natural immunity. Our reports show that it has gained in virulence and shortened its incubation period as it spread and the mortality is reported as one hundred percent of those it attacks. Only pneumonic plague has ever equaled its deadliness and that died out after a while. The great increase in density of populations and in transportation facilities in the past fifty years, plus the artificial stimulation to further spread, has made this disease far more horrible. As you know already, all travel off this continent is now halted and nobody is allowed to enter by sea until a compulsory quarantine period outside the three-mile limit has passed. Air traffic is under military orders. All troops and dependents overseas in threatened areas such as Korea, are already evacuated to quarantine zones in safe territory. A few members of advisory groups are staying behind, on a voluntary basis, to help our allies. Other garrisons, for example in Okinawa, are ready to leave."

There was a mixed reaction to this information, obvious in nods or shakes of heads.

"I realize this may leave our bases open to occupation by the enemy," the President continued, "but such would be open aggression and I do not believe they will risk it, especially if they think we are beaten already; they will be expecting to take over in their own good time." He stopped to drink from his water glass. "In the West we have a different problem. The enemy, hoping we would not be unduly alarmed by what seemed little worse than an epidemic of colds, infected us with sterility flu. The plan was to sterilize most of our male population before we became alert to the danger. It almost succeeded.

"I have the latest report from our public health authorities. It is estimated that eighty percent of the population of the United States and Canada has had, or will have, the S-Flu. Some twenty-five million people, both male and female, who are known to have escaped the disease, are at present protected either by weekly injections or by isolation, and we are searching vigorously for others. We hope in a few months time to have a vaccine which will give lasting protection. The combined police forces of both countries are searching night and day for the agents who, we suspect, are hiding in our cities, fanning the flu to fresh vigor whenever it shows signs of abating. If twenty percent do escape, since most of the females apparently do not become sterile, the future of our countries therefore will depend on the twenty million uninfected males. However, probably half of these are either too old or too young to be of use for procreation at this time. That leaves us with only ten million potential fathers north of the Rio Grande."

He paused to let this sink in and the buzz of conversation broke into excited comment. Tempers were getting short and here and there fists pounded the desks to emphasize a point. The chairman rapped for order and the President resumed as the noise died.

"The situation in Central and South America is worse. They do not have adequate facilities to protect their populations. Evidence is now coming in that S-Flu has also been let loose along with measlepox in the Orient so that those who escape the one and live may well have been sterilized by the other. The European countries have closed their borders in an attempt to keep the measlepox out. They are already overwhelmingly affected by the S-Flu.

"To sum up, except for the immunized master race of the USSR, the peoples of the world are either dead, dying or sterile. If ten percent escape one or the other fate we will be lucky. It might be considered that the war is already won, and so it is in the dying Orient, but we, although we are sterile, are still eager to fight...and fight we must if we are to save America and democracy for our children."

A roar of cheering drowned his attempt to continue. Senators, soldiers and members of parliament were up on their feet, yelling, cursing, banging desks or releasing their anger in any way they could find.

"Give them the Hell bomb," yelled one.

"Send over our planes," a portly congressman screamed.

"Kill them all, the monsters."

"It was terrific," Hallam broke off his recitation to comment. "I was sure several of those old cobbers would have a heart attack, they were so mad. Then somebody cut off the microphones and the noise became bearable. Finally the

President managed to get their attention and we all sat down again and listened."

"Your response is most heartening," the President resumed, "and just what I expected. However I want to make one point clear now. I, and Mr. Macpherson agrees with me, do not believe that the H-bomb or any other ordinary form of war is the answer to this for two reasons.

"Firstly, we have only a small fertile population left on which to rebuild our nations. The radiation effects of nuclear warfare might well turn those children of the future into misshapen monsters. We would have revenge at the cost of self-destruction. Secondly, this is still an undeclared war. The Reds are probably counting on victory and do not know that we are aware of their villainy. They will not expect a counter-attack as long as we pretend ignorance. It is up to us to deliver one that will catch them too by surprise. If we succeed we turn what appears to be inevitable defeat into victory. At the same time we must direct our efforts into other channels and find ways in which to maintain our strength in manpower as well as in machines.

"For our first task—that is, the winning of the war, I believe we must remember the old saying, fight fire with fire. Our best hope is in utilizing our own scientists to produce biological or chemical weapons, which will do to the Communists what they have done to us. For the second task I believe we will need new laws and new concepts of human behavior. We will have an opportunity, unequalled in history, to determine the future quality of our citizens. Let us go to this task full of confidence in our ability and thankful the Creator has allowed us another chance."

"After the President spoke," Hallam continued, "there was an explosion of applause, cheering, hand-clapping, shouting, whistling. It was long minutes before Mr. Macpherson could get their attention. He pledged Canada's full cooperation. In turn, the Commonwealth observers promised to get the help of their governments. Finally, committees were formed and the details of the President's broad concepts hashed out. Not every problem was settled right then, of course; that will take months, but the preliminary decisions were made."

"That's about the size of it," Hallam drained his glass, "except for what we are to do. Since we have been working on the S-Flu, we are to keep on, but with a different goal. We now have to build up a virus of our own with either a sterility factor or lethal properties and a very short incubation period."

"That's what the President meant by turning their weapons against them," Pat said.

"That is part of it," Hallam agreed. "It is axiomatic that this new virus must be far enough from the old one that there is little or no cross immunity, so that the vaccine the Reds took will not protect them."

"A tall order," I said glumly, "and while we try to do it, we hope the Commies will sit still, convinced that we are not suspicious of them."

"Like any murderers," Hallam said, "the Russians have to wait to see if the police suspect them. In the meantime, if they are smart, they won't draw suspicion on themselves by trying to profit from their crime. If my reasoning is correct, they may sit tight long enough for our surprise counterattack to work."

"You said there were several committees, didn't you?" Pat questioned him. "Have you any idea what other plans were made?"

"There are many lines of attack open," the Chief replied. "The Departments of Agriculture of our countries have been working on B.W. for some time, as it concerns plants and animals. If we could ruin Russian crops or kill their animals it might force them to capitulate from starvation. The weather experts are studying ways of doing the same thing by droughts, storms and so on. And of course the physicists think of such things as causing radioactive clouds over Siberia. The trouble is, we don't want to make the Reds suspicious too soon, or give them an excuse for starting all out atomic warfare, or even so called conventional war. Our people are close to extinction now, with only ten million breeding males. It seems like a lot but unless they are protected, we are finished."

"What's to be done about this sterility problem?" Polly spoke up.

"There's bound to be a lot of discussion and some bitter arguments on that," Hallam smiled at her. "There are about thirty million women of childbearing age in the United States and Canada, of whom roughly twenty million might be from sweet sixteen to a very desirable thirty or so," he grinned at the girls as he talked and they laughed.

"O.K. that's us," Polly said, "the or-so gals."

Hallam continued, "And only ten million more or less desirable but presumably still potent males from say eighteen to fifty or so." He saw Pat's mischievous smile and added, "Yes, that's me." He went back to his thesis. "Only five million of these would be of compatible age to marry the younger women, assuming nobody is married right now. If we could forget age differences, it means one man to every three women of childbearing age. The problem is much more complicated, as you can imagine, since many of these fertile men are already married and many more women, who could bear children, are married to sterile males. If we were Muslims or old-time Mormons, it might be possible to start harems of fertile people but with our present customs that's impossible."

"Rough on the sterile males," I said smugly, "but mighty nice for the rest. What are we going to do—wear a badge or something?" I stopped in sudden realization; Harry had had the flu. He sat there silently, his face impassive. The only thing to do was to carry on.

"Get that smirk off your face," Pat ordered. "You aren't a free agent any more."

"Sometimes I envy you real bachelors, Chief," I said, and sighed deeply in mock despair.

Hallam chuckled and then said seriously. "If we sit and do nothing the population will drop off drastically as the old folks die but eventually, in a normal situation, the race would renew itself. It might be a good thing too, we have too many people now, except for one thing...we need continuing manpower to beat the Communists."

He stopped to consider his next point. "To me, the logical solution is legal artificial insemination, voluntary of course, with sperm from carefully selected donors. In that way we would have less of a population drop and, I believe, improve the quality of the race; but it's a highly controversial question from scientific, legal and religious points of view. The committee will take some time and a lot of hearings before making even tentative decisions."

He stopped, and for a moment we were silent, thinking about our problems. Pat spoke first, "I keep remembering how we became aware of the S. factor...I mean when that ferret aborted. I wonder if we could use that as our weapon. If all the farm animals and women in Russia were unable to conceive, or miscarry when they did, it would do the trick...and it's a lot harder to determine whether a female is sterile than it is in a man."

"You have a possibility," I admitted. "Sometimes it's better to hit an enemy with a variation of his own favorite trick than to have an entirely new approach. If we could do that, we might fool the Reds into thinking something had gone wrong with their own S-Flu virus, such as another mutation. The difficulty is to avoid cross-immunity. We might do better to alter the measlepox so it would turn on them and kill them."

"Then you have lost the element of uncertainty that made the S-Flu so valuable a weapon," Polly said. "They could rally in time to stop it."

"A very good point." Harry spoke for the first time.

Again there was silence. I got up quietly to refill the glasses. Harry was staring at the fire; his face in the flickering light seemed tired and sad. I caught Polly watching him and saw the look of concern in her face and the faint wrinkle of perplexity between those artistically darkened eyebrows. The Chief was sunk down in his chair, in a daze partly of thought and partly of satiety. Absently he lifted his glass for a refill and then, looking through the deep red port to the firelight, he said to the room.

"The U.S. Navy is sending a special research team out to Formosa and the Army one to Japan, to study measlepox. Years ago they established well equipped research laboratories in those countries. The Canadian government wants one to go to Hong Kong."

Pat threw a quick glance at me but said nothing as he went on.

"They asked me for suggestions and I told them I'd take the team, but the Premier put his veto on that. He won't let me go. I objected to married men because it's likely to be dangerous work, at least until we get enough of the Russian vaccines to inoculate our men."

"When do they go?" I said.

"The advance parties should leave in a fortnight."

"Somebody should go from here, and since you can't go, that means me."

I had no wish to be a hero but there is a certain pride in a man. Our laboratory was the biggest, and I thought the best, virus research center in Canada. Somebody obviously had to do the dirty work if we were to be saved from destruction. Sooner or later the measlepox would invade the Americas or be brought in deliberately by the Reds. To paraphrase the old saying, as they wouldn't "let George do it," and as George was my boss, I was next in line.

The Chief was nodding his head in reluctant agreement as these thoughts ran in my head.

"Hold on a minute, there," Harry had come out of his trance and the sadness in his face was replaced by the excited, determined look of the volunteer, the man with an ideal. "This job is mine, it has to be!"

Polly was staring at him, her mouth half open, her drink stopped on the way to her lips. She put it down and spread her hands in appeal.

"I declare, the man's just naturally crazy," she said to Pat.

"They both are," Pat muttered angrily.

None of the men paid any attention.

"Why so, Harry?" Dr. Hallam asked.

"Sir, I've never said much about my parents except that they were medical missionaries in China and that I grew up there before the Second World War. You knew that, didn't you?"

The Chief nodded in agreement.

"Well, there's one point in my favor. I speak several Chinese dialects and can work without an interpreter. If we go to the mainland I know my way about, too. And I know enough virology to do field work."

Hallam nodded again. "That's true enough."

"But that's not all. I have a personal score to settle with the Reds and by God, here's my chance!" He leaned forward and almost spat the words right into Hallam's astonished eyes. Seeing Harry get angry was something like seeing an iceberg suddenly spout fire.

"I told you that my parents were missionaries in China. What I didn't tell you is that they never got out!"

He stopped. The rush of angry words from his flushed face died away into the room. In my mind they echoed again. "They never got out...never got out...never." We waited. The soft rustle of the flames seemed loud as their shadows wavered on the circle of still faces, all eyes were riveted on Harry.

More quietly now, his face once more almost its impassive self, he went on.

"They stayed with the Chinese Nationalist Forces all through the world war and afterwards, when the Communists took over, they were lost. When I was demobbed from the British Army I went to Hong Kong but I couldn't trace them and I couldn't get back into China. Some of the refugees I met thought they'd been executed for aiding the anticommunists...mostly their own converts to Christianity, but there was no proof. That's why I came over here to work when I ran out of money. Vancouver is the closest main port to the Orient and I hoped I might keep in touch while I made a living. Now I know they are almost certainly dead…and I want a chance to do something to beat those Red pigs."

His voice rose again on the last sentence and he looked straight at the Director. Hallam had sunk deep into his chair, again, his eyes shaded behind the heavy rims of his glasses.

"I see…I see now," he murmured. "Yes, you must have your chance."

I looked over at Polly. Her eyes were wet and her lower lip looked suspiciously tight. She said nothing as Pat put a warm arm around her shoulders.

Harry was staring again at the fire. He was not here. Somewhere in China, or maybe nowhere in this world, was the red hell he saw in the flames.

CHAPTER NINE

THE Ides of March, as I like to call the month, were upon us. Once in a while the sun peered through the heavy clouds, sliding its pale beams between their tumbling banks to reach the soggy earth. Then came a night of rain, of heavy wind and thrashing trees; a faint rumbling of thunder over the sea and the mountains. I woke up and lay listening to the water as it dripped on the balcony while Pat, in troubled sleep, muttered and moved beside me. I woke again to a bright, cloudless sky, a perfect spring day.

After the routine checking of our animals and cultures, Dr. Hallam called a halt.

"Pat, you're tired," he said. "I think you're going stale."

"I'm slowed to a walk. It must be spring fever."

"It's spring all right," I said. "Look at that beautiful sunshine. It's time to shuck off the long woollies and take a big dose of sulphur and molasses."

"What a horrible thought," Pat grimaced, "Did you ever?"

"I sure did," I said. "My mother was the old-fashioned castor-oil-is-good-for-you type. She thought I needed a tonic to get the sap running every spring."

"The sap can run again…right out to Stanley Park," Hallam grinned, "and take Pat with you. She needs a rest and some fresh air. I'm going to play golf. We'll start again tomorrow."

We had reached a lull in our experiments. It was the obvious time for a break.

I drove slowly through the park until, in a grassy enclosure not far from Brockton Point, we found the seclusion we wanted. In midweek, at that time of day, we had the place almost to ourselves. I put down a groundsheet, opened the car blanket on it, and we lay down. The mild sea breeze rustled soothingly in my ears and brought with it the faint splashing of the tide against the jumbled boulders of the shore. A deep-sea ship hooted at the Lion's Gate bridge and, like an echo, the answering call gave it clearance to pass. For a moment more I lay still but the bustle of life around me was too strong to allow relaxation and I sat up to look out over the harbor. I turned to Pat as she lay quietly beside me. The wind had settled her dress closely to her parted legs. I followed the clean lines upward, and when I got to her eyes I saw that she had been watching me. They sparkled with amusement.

"Like what you see, huh?" she teased me.

"Love it, darling," I replied and leaned over for a kiss.

She broke it off before I was through and as I backed away I saw the slight frown that deepened the lines above her nose.

"What's the matter?"

"Nothing much, I hope. A slight pain in my stomach." She used the word in the ordinary sense.

"Whereabouts?"

"Low down above the pubis. It's gone now."

I laid my hand on the lower part of her belly and palpated it softly. There was no rigidity, no unusual mass.

"Does that hurt?" I probed deeper.

"No, it's a little uncomfortable, that's all."

I thought momentarily of the various possibilities and then dismissed it. The day was too lovely to spoil with a clinical discussion.

"Something you ate, no doubt." I smiled at her and lowered my mouth to touch her full red lips gently, once again.

She pushed me away. "That's enough. This place is too public."

I studied the bold contour of her nose and concluded that it was too large for true beauty...the French influence, no doubt, in her Louisiana heritage. Her attractiveness was in her expressions more than in physical structure, I decided, but the mouth was perfect, no doubt about that, and her grey eyes as clear as a mountain pool filtered through limestone. I snuggled close to her, contentedly, and was beginning to doze in the fresh warmth of the springtime air when I felt her body tighten. I opened my eyes and rested on one elbow, watching her.

"What is it baby, the pain again?"

"Yes, it's crampy now...something like a bad period," she twisted a little.

"Is it that time of the month again?"

"It could be. I've been having odd periods, very slight flow. I thought I might possibly be pregnant. It's been that way since I seduced you in December."

"That wasn't seduction, baby. That was merely anticipating the inevitable."

I began to question her seriously. There was little doubt in my mind after a few minutes that, if she wasn't pregnant, she was not behaving as a normal woman should. While we talked the pain returned, cramping and severe. She went white and pressed her hands to her belly in search of relief. That ruined the day. I took her home immediately.

"Take your clothes off and lie on the bed. I want to examine you," I said when we got there.

When I had finished there wasn't much doubt. She was about three months pregnant and threatening to abort. I left her in bed while I washed my hands. Then I came back and told her. For a moment she tried to be brave but then the tears came and I held her tight while her sobs shook us both.

"I've been afraid something might happen," she said finally, after I'd wiped off her wet face with a towel.

I sat on the edge of the bed. "Why?"

"You know I've been working with female ferrets, infected from the original one that aborted, trying to find out if that virus was a mutant from the S-Flu."

"Yes, I know that."

"I've passed it through quite a few females now and it's been showing definite differences. A week ago, I transferred it again and the ferrets got sick. I was working with one three days ago and it got loose and jumped on my shoulder and sneezed and clawed me as I tried to get it down and put it back in its cage."

"You had your suit on, didn't you?"

"Of course I did, but after I came out of the shower I noticed a little dampness. I checked the suit and found a defective shoulder seam where the helmet joins on. I suppose the ferret's claws opened it up. With all that movement I could have sucked some infected air into the suit."

"I don't know. With a separate air supply it doesn't seem too likely unless the claws carried virus inside like a hypodermic injection. It didn't scratch you did it?"

"A little bit, I think, but it was on a place where I couldn't see it. I washed it with disinfectant later."

"Oh my God, what next?" I exclaimed. "But you've been having some irregular bleeding before this. Maybe it would have happened anyway. You don't have any signs of the flu?"

"I feel a bit stuffy and aching as if I were getting a cold."

"Well, we'll see. You rest here while I figure out what to do."

The fact that this might be the mutation we were looking for didn't penetrate just then. All I cared about was that Pat was sick and I had to take care of her, if possible, without a scandal. I was standing beside the bed, my mind racing over the various possibilities when she groaned and whispered, "John, the pain is really bad now. I think I'm bleeding too."

I got her a couple of codeine tablets and then dialed the Chief. This was one situation I couldn't handle myself, for obvious reasons, and I needed someone with understanding and discretion.

He was there in less than fifteen minutes, fortunately having just returned to the clubhouse when I called. He heard my report. He checked Pat himself. She was well along now and we both agreed that there was no chance of stopping the miscarriage.

"Have you been close to many other people in the last three days?" he asked her, looking very disturbed.

"Nobody but you and John, as far as I know," she gasped between spasms of pain.

It was probably true. We three were working on the secret problems in isolation during the day. Polly and Harry helped us with the procedures that had to be done in the main lab and so were not in direct physical contact with us. We seldom stopped work until long after the day workers had left the Lab and were there in the morning before them. We didn't go out for meals during the day as we had all we needed on the top floor. I could see Hallam was concerned about the disease getting loose. If the vaccine we had was no protection from this new mutation, and if Pat had a case of flu it obviously wasn't, then this new disease could raise hell among the people and maybe finish what the Reds had started.

"We can't stay here, and we can't take her to a hospital," the Chief decided. "We mustn't let this new virus get out. I'll have to take care of her myself in the Research Lab. There are some instruments there and we can get more if we need them." He looked down at Pat. "I'm no obstetrician, my dear, but I think we can see you through this if you agree."

Pat smiled tiredly. "You're a doctor, and a good one. Do what you think best."

I had to agree even though it frightened me. I'd seen dozens of similar cases in my earlier days as a young intern but my imagination was too active where my own loved ones were concerned. The main danger was sudden hemorrhage but we could easily get blood sent up to us. Otherwise nature would probably take care of things in its own way. By now it was after rush hour and the Lab would be empty. Once more we let ourselves into the building and went up to the top floor, using the elevator for Pat's sake. She could hardly walk by now, even with our help, and it was a struggle to get her to her room. Once there we stripped the bed down. I prepped her and draped her for delivery and the Chief gave her intravenous Demerol and a capsule of seconal. Then we waited.

An hour later it was over. She had aborted spontaneously, and, as far as we could tell, completely. With the assistance of a small dose of ergot we had controlled the bleeding and the uterus was small and firm. I checked her pulse and blood pressure. There was no sign of shock. She lay there quietly after I had changed the linen and, as I pulled the covers over her, she took my hand.

"I'm so sorry, John," she said weakly. "I guess I wrecked my own plans for having your baby when I got careless with that ferret. Now I'm probably sterile."

She began to cry silently, the big tears rolling slowly on to the pillow.

I stroked her damp hair back from her forehead and kissed her eyes gently. "Maybe you aren't sterile," I said hopefully, "and even if you are it doesn't matter. I love you, and I'll always love you, whether we have children or not."

"I wonder how many years we'll have to spend cooped up in here?" I said, half-seriously to Dr. Hallam later that night. Pat was sleeping soundly under the influence of a capsule of sodium amytal he had given her. We had cooked a steak dinner and now we sat, weary but relieved, over our coffee.

"Lord alone knows," he said. "We'll have to stay here now until we see if you and I are going to catch this thing and what the effects will be. I hope for the sake of our research project we do get it, although I'm not happy about being a guinea pig. Even if it proves to be a suitable weapon we still have to come up with a cure for it, or rather a vaccine to prevent it, so our own people and our allies are protected."

"Why include the allies?" I said, merely for the sake of argument. "Won't that increase the risk of the Reds learning our plans?"

"It will, unless we take a calculated risk. I believe we should manufacture vaccine and stockpile it, not to be issued until the disease is actually causing epidemics in Russia. Then we can fly the vaccine all over the world and let our friends use it. Some people may catch the disease, but not too many. We might even offer some to the Russians, to allay their suspicions, making sure it's too late to help much."

"But don't you think they'll get wise?"

"Of course! But if we do it right I believe they won't dare to use open aggression any more than we are doing."

"This kind of undeclared war could go on interminably, as the Cold War seemed to do back in the Fifties," I said gloomily.

"It probably could," Hallam agreed. "Our one hope is to effect a change in leaders, or at least in policy, in Russia. Maybe, just maybe, new leaders will arise who will work with the democracies for a world system of government."

"A faint hope," I said, "but I'll go to bed now before that cheerful thought yields to glum reality."

I checked Pat before I turned in. She was resting well and I thought she looked a little less feverish. Her head felt cooler and her pulse was about normal. Sadly, thinking of her loss and mine, I closed the door behind me.

Pat's recovery was rapid and uneventful. The following morning she got up and had coffee with us. In a couple of days she was getting around well although the Chief wisely insisted she rest for long periods and absolutely refused to let her work in the Lab. Part of her restless energy she expended on preparing tasty meals for us until we both began to grumble about our expanding waistlines. There was no sign that the new disease had ill effects other than what she had already suffered. Whether or not she was sterile was a question that would have to wait. I had no intention of putting it to the test for a good long time. To work for the cause of science was all very well but I could see no point in sacrificing my love to it.

The new virus was christened FS for female sterility and we re-named the old one MS for male sterility. The new one was easy to grow. It thrived on fertilized eggs, in ferrets, hamsters, mice and monkeys; in every animal we could find. With passage through numerous generations it became more virulent until, in its final form, it caused abortion in all pregnant animals. Invariably, after recovery of the animals, our pathologists were unable to find any developing eggs in their ovaries. Because of their short breeding cycle we worked mainly with hamsters, those fat little relatives of the guinea pig. Even the amazing fertility of the hamster was stopped by the FS virus.

"It looks as if we have the answer for the Russians," I said exultantly after we had tallied our results some weeks later.

"I'm not so sure, John, not so sure at all," Hallam said thoughtfully.

"Why is that, Sir?"

"Have you ever thought of the consequences of sterilizing every mammal on earth, and perhaps the birds and other animals too?" he asked. "This FS virus is powerful. If we start another pandemic it could get away from us. It might increase in power still more, though God knows it's bad enough. And obviously we can't inoculate every animal of all the species it may affect even when we find the vaccine to counteract it. We'd have to build another Noah's Ark and take it out in the middle of the ocean to be sure we could save them from extinction."

"We have a Noah's Ark now." I suggested. "We could isolate the Americans from Asia, Europe and Africa. Australia and New Zealand could do the same. We are doing it for the measlepox right now until there is enough vaccine to go around."

"That's true, although it wouldn't be difficult for the Russians to smuggle the virus ashore. They might do it if they thought they were licked. The dying soldier often tries to drag his enemy down with him.

"But aside from all that," he continued, "I still don't like it. Men have wiped out some of the most beautiful and interesting creatures of this earth. The passenger pigeon is gone. The bison is a curiosity in National Parks. The trumpeter swan is in danger and the California condor is on its last lap. I don't believe this world was created just so man could ruin it, and I don't want to go down in history as the most ruthless destroyer of all time. Oh, I know I'll be expected to give this discovery to our politicians. The discoverers of the atomic bomb and H-bomb did just that and their consciences have bothered them ever since. There is a greater loyalty in this world than loyalty to one's country…it is loyalty to the human race. I believe in the Golden Rule. Call it Christian logic if you wish. We have already disturbed the balance of Creation in this world as a cancer disturbs the human body, and, like a cancer, when we destroy too much of the world we too may die."

"But the Russians don't live and let live," I objected. "Are you willing to let them take over the world and perpetuate communist doctrines?"

"It's a thought I do not like," he said very quietly, "but all through history "isms" have grown and then have died as time passed. This "ism" too could pass. Perhaps Gandhi was right. Passive resistance won in India and although the Reds are much more cruel than the British ever were, even they can't go too far. Remember the East German revolt and the Georgian riots after the denunciation of Stalin? Remember the horrors of Hungary? Our agents report increasing unrest in Russia itself. The people are sick of repression and terror. Demands for moderation are even printed in their papers. The Far Left is slowly moving back to the middle of the road. We should go to meet it instead of edging farther and farther to the Right, into the nightmare world of Hitler and Mussolini."

"Then what are we to do? Do you want to destroy the virus?"

"I don't know. After all, you and Pat are involved in this and may not agree."

"I know the politicians would want us to give them the information," I said. "I'll never forget in the States during the row over the H-bomb and Oppenheimer, how some pompous ass of a senator got up and said he thought scientists should stick to science and leave decisions of ethics and national policy to those who knew best—meaning himself and those like him. Democracy is a wonderful thing but I can't see how getting elected makes any man a sage. I honestly doubt if the ordinary politician is as competent to judge the effects of a scientific discovery as the scientists themselves are."

"What about democracy and the will of the majority?" Hallam countered.

"You have me there," I admitted. "I suppose if we adhere strictly to that idea there should be a vote on whether or not to use this new weapon, which, of course, would lose us the element of surprise. But again, what does the ordinary man know about such things. To come right down to it...how often has there been a nation-wide vote in any democratic country on whether or not to get into a war?"

"I know of none," Hallam answered, "which means of course that essentially, in times of stress, decisions are made by a few, or even by one man. And that brings us full circle. Shall we make the decision now?"

"I feel somewhat like the old country doctor who taught me obstetrics," I said. "Whenever he was in doubt about a delivery he sat down, lit a big cigar, and waited. Nature usually took care of things for him."

"A smart idea," said the boss. "We'll work—and wait."

CHAPTER TEN

TOWARDS the end of April the Canadian research team left for Hong Kong. Now that inter-continental air traffic had ceased, Sea Island was quieter than usual, but even so, the roar of engines warming up in the cold dawn made it difficult to hear. Out on the tarmac the big RCAF jet transport rolled ponderously behind its tractor, wings drooping like a great eagle hovering over its nest. It glided silently to the loading area and we moved, a small knot of people, to where we could watch and wait for the word to embark.

"I hope Hong Kong will be warmer than this, Harry," I said, shivering deeper into my trench coat as the cold dawn wind crawled up my sleeves and down my neck.

"April is usually very pleasant," he said. "It's after the winter and before the rains."

"I was there a couple of times after the Korean War. I imagine the Kowloon side is cut off now. Used to be some nice shopping centers there."

"I don't suppose there'll be much left," he replied. "The area has been isolated for months. Everybody who could get away has gone. I expect it will be more like a prison camp than a tourist resort."

"Well, it shouldn't be too bad," I grinned at him. "Some of those Chinese girls with the high split skirts were mighty nice looking."

"Hush up now, you hear?" Polly said. "Don't you be giving him ideas."

"I don't need to Polly, he's been there before."

"Don't pay any attention to John," Pat said. "His mind's in a rut."

"Can you think of a better one?" Hallam asked.

"Oh, you men!" Polly snorted contemptuously.

"The luggage is all loaded, Doctor," a young RCAF officer had come up and reported to Cope. "We're ready to go now."

"Thank you," Harry said and turned to the Chief. "I'll let you know what happens, sir."

"Take care of yourself, boy," Dr. Hallam said as they shook hands.

We turned away, leaving him alone with Polly. In a few minutes she rejoined us, chattering brightly in her usual animated fashion until the plane moved out to the runway and Harry could no longer see us. Then her composure cracked and she cried. Pat and I took her to our place where the two girls buzzed around making breakfast and keeping themselves busy until the shock of parting had worn off a bit for Polly. Over our second cup of coffee she started to talk about it.

"It's a strange thing to say but I'm glad Harry's gone. I just know he never would have been happy with me if he hadn't done it."

"Why do you think that?" I asked.

"He never did tell me much about his people...no more than he told you all. I knew he was holding out on me but it wasn't any of my business. These English people don't brag much about themselves and their families. Anyway I knew he felt real bad when he got the S-Flu because as soon as he knew he was sterile he tried to tell me to go find somebody else. He seemed to think because he couldn't give me children I wouldn't want him. I told him I didn't hanker to marry a stud horse but it didn't do much good. I guess having no mother and father and then losing his chance to have kids of his own made him feel low. Maybe this will get it out of his head and he'll be OK," she paused, "that is, if he ever comes back. Somehow I feel deep down that he won't."

"Oh, don't be silly, Polly," Pat shut her up. "You got up too early this morning. Here, have some more hot coffee."

With the coming of spring across the cold northern continents, the big counter-offensive had begun. For years the agricultural scientists had prepared for such an occasion and now they went into action. Naturally it was all top secret but we were among the privileged few, since the borderline between the world of plant pathology and the diseases of man and animals had grown increasingly vague. It was essential that we know of their work and they of ours. Many of the original discoveries in virology had been made by botanical scientists and the first virus to be crystallized, the tobacco mosaic, was a disease confined to the plant world.

Since the Geophysical Year of 1958 and the advent of the space satellites, the meteorologists had made tremendous advances. Using information derived from the weather globes circling the earth, with their data on sunspots and radar maps of storm centers, plus the mass of information now available through the weather stations in the polar regions, at sea and on land, the weather predictors had become extremely accurate. With seeding techniques, electronically controlled, they had made a start at changing the weather, although, up to now, little of this had been done because of a lack of international agreements. Now they were free to tryout their ideas. It was interesting to follow in the newspapers the results of their work, and even more interesting to see how the peoples of the world tried to explain the various events. The great pandemics raging across the earth had resulted in a rush to the churches and the rise of all sorts of weird sects, prophets and calamity howlers. This frantic search for security renewed itself when the new wave of disaster began. To avert suspicion, for a while at least, and also because these great forces could not easily be localized, our NATO allies had to suffer with the Communists. Only the heads of the British Government knew, and they, with their usual courage, had agreed to endure, with the promise of American aid.

The first attack was a weather offensive. Using the jet streams, which flowed swiftly to the east, swarms of tiny balloons were released by planes from the American Navy supercarriers in the Atlantic, and from the bombers of the Strategic Air Command cruising in the stratosphere above them. By the use of timing devices these deadly little toys destroyed themselves and dropped the new electronic seeders into the moisture-filled clouds rolling from the Atlantic across Europe. The wettest spring in recorded history was the result. Fields were almost untillable and the hay and grain crops that were planted were never harvested. The wet weather favored the growth of fungus and the rusts and blights so carefully cultivated by our agronomists and seeded into the winds that blew over Europe and Asia, thrived on what remained of the harvest. Further to the east the winds, now emptied of their moisture, sucked water from the steppes of Siberia, where the great new collective farms ordered by Khrushchev had torn up the grasslands. Dust storms scoured off the topsoil. No plants could grow. No animal could survive, lacking both food and water. The greatest migration in living memory was the result. The trek of the Okies out of the dust bowl of the early thirties was a mere trickle compared to the flood of refugees that poured east into Russia or south, down into the desert lands of the Middle East and over the Himalayan barriers. Many died before they got to the borders of India and the other Islamic lands. Many were killed by the reinforced border guards determined to prevent the spread of disease and famine in their own ravaged territories.

Of course the Communists retaliated, or perhaps it was in part the result of our own interference with nature. That fall, early frost hit the West Coast and blizzards screamed down from the Arctic over the plains. Our grain crops were ruined and much of our late fruit and vegetables. And now the "Folly of the Fifties", as one presidential candidate had called the price support programs, paid an unexpected dividend. From every cave and warehouse, from dumps and silos and refrigerator rooms, the stores of grain and potatoes, butter and meat, poured out by truck and train. Convoys of food ships had already left for the NATO countries. The terrible death toll of the measlepox made available sufficient food for the rice eaters of the Indian subcontinent from their existing supplies, since the weather war had had little effect in those regions. Africa, its own population decimated by the same measlepox disease, was left to its rich resources.

The Reds were not yet beaten. Desperate for food, they gambled boldly. The Soviet premier himself appealed to the United States and Canada for aid, in a shrewd psychological move. He knew we did not want to announce to the world that we were at war. It was doubtful if even our own people would believe it. World opinion would be likely to turn against us and uninformed or unbelieving governments, side with the Communists to isolate us. We had to help them, at least in appearance. In spite of tremendous losses the Soviets still outnumbered us and, if pushed too far, might start the long-awaited march into the vacuum left by the dying populations of Asia and the evacuation of our bases, daring us to start an all-out war.

The counterstroke was a masterpiece. Supplies of flour and other prepared foods were rushed, in great fleets of ships, to the European ports of the Russian Empire. Every pound of flour, every ton of meat, every cask of butter had been treated with the new tasteless and odorless contraceptive compound, which our scientists had recently discovered. We never knew if the Russians found out why their women were not getting pregnant...the rate of conception drops off in starvation in any case. It did not matter. They had two choices, to eat or to die.

In June, six weeks after he had left Sea Island, we heard again from Harry. Of course Polly had had letters, but purely personal ones as Harry had been much too busy to do more than write, "I love you, wish you were here" notes. Now, finally, he gave us some news. Polly came bursting into the coffee room one morning waving a sheaf of electron pictures in one hand and a bundle of closely written pages in the other.

"I got a big letter from Harry this morning," she said to the three of us around the table. "Would y'all like to hear the news?"

"Aw Polly, I don't want to hear that mush," I kidded her. "Why don't you sell it to True Love Confessions magazine?"

"You shut your big mouth, man, and open your ears."

"Go ahead Polly. Never mind funny boy here," Pat said.

"Harry says they have a big lab set up in the main hospital in Victoria...that's the city on the island, Hong Kong itself, and they're working shifts, twenty-four hours a day, to try to attenuate the measlepox virus."

"Brother! What a job!" I exclaimed. "One mistake and you've had it."

"Too right, you have!" the Chief said feelingly, his long forgotten Australian slang coming to the surface.

"They had to get out of Kowloon, he says because the refugees sneaked through the barriers into the New Territories and spread the disease. It was terrible because there were about three million people crowded in there. Now most of them are dead and the police patrol all around the island, day and night, to keep others from landing. He says almost all the British, except soldiers, have left. They send them to some small island first and then, if they haven't got any disease, they can go home to England. The research team is behind barbed wire and almost nobody is allowed in or out—but their quarters are comfortable."

"Hot and cold running maids, I suppose," I said.

"If you were there they'd be running, all right."

"Shut up, John. Go on Polly," Pat said and pinched my arm.

"They haven't succeeded in weakening the virus yet and if they kill it with formalin or one of the usual methods it won't work as a vaccine."

"What ways have they tried?" Hallam said.

"He doesn't say. There's one thing I don't like," she said thoughtfully. "He has an idea that if they went into China they might find survivors of the pox in areas where the disease has almost died down and get some serum from them, or perhaps find that the measlepox is weakened in those areas and could be used."

"It's too bad our agents didn't get enough vaccine for testing," I said. "It would have saved exposing our men to that sort of danger."

"One of his ideas is to give volunteers serum from recovered cases and then let them get the measlepox."

"You mean like giving children gamma globulin shots after they've been exposed to measles so they'll get just a mild case of the disease and be protected for life?" Pat asked.

"That's the general idea," the Chief said. "Then, too, he might want to look at the animal population in the area. There's a theory that cowpox was originally smallpox that got into cattle. Now if you get cowpox, as milkmaids in England often did many years ago, on their hands, you probably won't catch smallpox. That's how the legend arose that milkmaids had lovely complexions. They didn't get smallpox and so their faces weren't scarred like most people in the eighteenth century. Jenner got the original idea for vaccination from that. The same thing might apply to measlepox. If he could find a mild form of it in some animal we could use that as a vaccine. We try to do this in the Lab by inoculating animals. Harry wants to go out into the devastated areas and see if nature has done it for him."

"That may be soon, Doctor," Polly said, "but I'll bet he's also hoping to pick up news of his folks."

"Could be," Hallam agreed, "but they are very small pins in a terribly big haystack, if still alive."

"That crazy man," Polly murmured. "I know he'll kill himself yet. If he doesn't get the pox the Reds will catch him."

"There's not too much danger from the Chicoms right now," I said. "The way they are dying out, the border guard must have holes in it big enough to take a division of troops through, let alone a small reconnaissance party."

In the early summer of 1963 Pat had completely recovered from her miscarriage. The Chief and I had suffered nothing more than mild colds from the FS-flu. We had set up new experiments to see if we could temper the destructiveness of the virus with the intention of confining its effects to the human race.

"I have no compunction about using it on the human race," Hallam said. "The human being has free will and should be prepared to take the consequences of his follies and work out his own salvation."

I had to agree.

One late summer day when the tests were running smoothly he said to me, "John, I think you should take Pat out of here for a month. There's no point in isolation now we are all recovered, and you need a rest."

"What about you?" I said.

"I'll take a break after you get back. Besides, I want you to do a little experimenting on your vacation."

I wondered out loud what was coming next.

"Well," he smirked, "this is a good chance for a honeymoon and you might find out for me how permanent the sterility effects of the original FS-flu are.

I couldn't think of a more pleasant experiment.

The United Church ceremony was a quiet one. Both Pat and I felt that, having been married before and having subsequently made fools of ourselves, we didn't want much fuss this time. The ceremony was quiet but the party that followed certainly was not. Dr. Hallam had recently moved into a penthouse apartment in the swanky new Lion Heights district overlooking Howe Sound and the Straits of Georgia. From the church it was a quick run out to his home, followed all the way by the hooting automobiles of half the Laboratory staff and a good crowd from the Hospital itself.

From the corner living room of the apartment there was a magnificent view south to Point Grey and the University. Off to the southwest, in the haze of late afternoon, the Olympic mountains glimmered faintly across the water and the dark silhouette of the Island cut the western horizon. To escape for a moment from the uproar, I had moved out onto the rooftop garden and, with my arm around Pat, watched the slow ending of the day. Behind us the French doors opened as Hallam joined us. The buzz of talk and laughter, heightened by the cocktails, broke the quiet of our thoughts and died again as he closed the doors behind him.

"This really is a lovely spot," Pat said to him, "Will you pardon a woman's curiosity and tell me, isn't it terribly expensive?"

Hallam grinned. "It would be except that I'm part owner of the building and get a cut rate."

We stood there quietly, absorbed in the view, then Pat took Hallam's arm. "Let's go in now," she said. "We will have to leave soon."

The noise came at us in waves as we opened the door. Little knots of people were all over the rooms, talking, laughing, eating, moving about and re-forming new groups.

"They obviously don't need us," I whispered to Pat. "Let's get out of here." I winked at the boss and he shook both hands to us, prizefighter fashion, as we slipped out.

The Ferguson glided into the driveway without the motor running as I tried to escape. A roar of hand clapping, cheers, jeers and yells broke out above. It was too late for them to catch us so they waved and shouted words of tipsy wisdom. A few ribald male remarks were stifled by feminine hands and the last howls and shrieks faded back up the hill. At the bottom I stopped and removed the inevitable tin cans and old shoes, brushed off all visible confetti and moved on towards Horseshoe Bay. The sloop was ready. While I started the motor and cast off, Pat changed into slacks and sweater in the cabin and then got busy making sandwiches and coffee. I set our course around Bowen Island, heading for the Sunshine Coast and the long winding fiords that split the timbered ranges.

It was hours later. At Pat's suggestion I had gone below for a rest and then had relieved her while she did the same. We wanted to get well away from the big city and the ocean traffic before we stopped. About two o'clock she wandered up from below. The moon was high now and in the clean cool light we were close to shore. Here the coast was deserted and, as we skirted a rocky point, a small cove appeared, the entrance barely large enough for the yacht. The moon, going over to the west, shot its light through the gap to show a sandy beach dimly outlined at the farther side.

"John, let's look in there. It seems a likely place to stop."

I cut the motor and glided through the entrance, trusting the smooth unbroken surface to cover enough depth for the boat. The million pinpoint lights of our phosphorescent track died away as we slowed. The bowsprit almost overhung the sloping beach when I dropped anchor.

"Plenty of depth here," I said quietly, reluctant to break the silence. "It should be a good spot to spend the night."

Sheltered by the northern arm of the cove, the remains of an old cabin hugged the rising slope. In front of it, in the little clearing, a few old fruit trees, branches broken with age, spotted the grass. The small stream that probably had tempted this early settler ran at one side of the cleared land, the water spreading out to glitter over the stones and sand of the beach before losing itself in the dark salty bay.

"What a wonderful place for a swim," Pat whispered, her eyes enormous in her shadowed face.

The air was still warm, with enough breeze to discourage any mosquitoes.

Quickly Pat stripped and stood there proudly, waiting for me. To keep her hair dry she had put on a white bathing cap and, in that pale light, she shone like some strange shaven statue from an old Egyptian tomb. She moved and the illusion disappeared. Naked, I reached for her and pulled her close. For a moment she clung to me and then, teasingly, she pushed me away and dived over the side. The water was cold and the chill of it on my skin soon relieved the tension the sight of her body had aroused in me. For a while we swam and splashed in the shallows, then I loaded the dinghy with towels and blankets, threw in a flask of rum with some cokes to dilute it and we went ashore. Her hand in mine, we walked around the tiny cove, the sand coming up pleasantly between our toes and the cool salty water sparkling on our skins. I brushed it out of my hair and Pat shivered as the fine spray hit her bare skin.

"Better get warmed up," I said, and led her back to the clearing.

There, from a deep pool dug in the stream by that early settler, I poured fresh water over her and rubbed vigorously with my hands to get off the salt and warm her up. The throbbing aching torment of my desire returned. She moved closer, her tongue wet on my lips.

In the soft grey glow of late moonlight, her face, twisted for a time by the agony of her passion, was smiling calm and her eyes looked up at me serenely. I rolled away from her and pulled the blanket over us. She cuddled into my shoulder and slept.

CHAPTER ELEVEN

THE sunny days slid by as we explored farther and farther north. The weather held fair all that month except for a few quick showers that washed the warm decks and cooled the quiet air. There was little good sailing weather but we didn't worry. There was fishing enough, swimming enough, and loving enough to fill the days and nights.

In a deep side channel of Louise Inlet, I was trolling one day in the fourth week. Pat held the tiller and the engine, throttled back hard, barely puttered along. Then, above the noise, the sound of a more powerful engine rose and gained rapidly in intensity. Around the bend from the main channel an amphibian swung into view and banked to glide down over us. It banked again, full circle, and the pilot let down and taxied up behind our boat. I stopped the engine and waited. The small door on the passenger side opened and a bare head stuck out. I recognized that full, cheery face.

"For the love of Pete! It's the Chief," I yelled above the motor.

Pat nodded, not too happily. Her woman's intuition was probably working overtime. A short time later we anchored inshore. The Boss and his grim-looking pilot climbed aboard.

"Lord, we've had a time finding you two," Hallam sighed. "This is Colonel Jones, United States Air Force."

I raised my eyebrows at Pat. Neither the man's flying suit nor the plane's markings had shown any indication of their military nature.

"How do you do sir," I said, as I shook his hand. "Are you up here on a vacation?"

"Strictly business, I'm afraid," he said crisply.

"Business? With whom?"

"With you." The lips opened and shut in his face like a ventriloquist's dummy.

He was strictly business, I thought. "With me?" I turned to Hallam. "What have I done now?"

He didn't smile at my feeble joke. "It's not what you've done, John, it's what they want you to do. Colonel Jones is from the CIA."

"Oh oh, the cloak and dagger boys," I thought. "Trouble coming up." Out loud I said, "We might as well sit down and be comfortable while we talk. Pat, how about some beer?"

The Colonel was obviously impatient but he tried to swallow his irritability with his beer.

"It's nice being a civilian at times," I was thinking. "I don't have to take any more guff from the brass. This guy's obviously a West Point type in a hurry and it must gall him to have to wait on my royal pleasure. He wants something. Let him wait for it!"

It was a rebellious thought but I'd been prodded painfully by his classmates on occasion in the past. I couldn't resist getting a little of my own back.

"All three of you are cleared for Top Secret," Jones said. "I checked before I came out here."

I took a long drag at the bottle. "What about yourself, Colonel?" I smiled thinly at him.

Silently, stone-faced, he showed his credentials. Pat frowned at me. She thought I was being unnecessarily cool to a guest. Rivalries in the service meant nothing to her.

I grinned at him and the tension eased. "The old routine, Colonel. I wouldn't want to foul up with a security officer watching me."

The stern exterior cracked as he relaxed. "I hate to butt in on your vacation like this. I had no choice. We have a deadline to meet."

"Sounds familiar," I murmured. "Submit a complete report, in five copies, based on information you'll get tomorrow, to reach headquarters not later than yesterday. Well, give us the bad news."

"First let me give you an estimate of the situation as we see it. That will put you in the picture."

"You mean I'm being framed?" I joked.

He actually smiled. "The weather and biological offensive against the Reds are now at their height," he began, "and are proving most successful. We anticipate they will exhaust their food reserves very soon and will be desperate for more. If they ask us, we will give them some this winter, under certain conditions." (He was referring to the use of the contraceptive drug in that food, as I learned later.) "That will give them a respite, which we can't very well avoid, and the war is expected to continue on into 1964. By early summer, some eight months from now, we estimate that continuation of our offensive will drive them to the wall, since we will then inform them that we cannot give them any more supplies from our store. It is then that we can anticipate the hidden war breaking out into the open. Even if they retaliate in weather and bacteriological warfare, they must know we can win because our hoarded supplies will keep us going while they starve. They have to plan a knockout blow and yet our G-2 people believe they will not use atomic power. They won't use it because of its dreadful after-effects on future populations. Even the so-called clean bombs must affect many survivors and, in an already decimated world, they cannot afford to have contaminated survivors from which to rebuild the race. Also, they are sure that we won't use it if they don't. Now, as far as we can foresee, that leaves only one other way to achieve the knockout…by the use of nerve gases."

"But we have nerve gases too."

"Yes, of course. However, we have information from our agents in Russia that, as a last desperate chance, they will fire their intercontinental missiles, plus shorter range rockets from their submarine fleet, at every major population center and key military target in the U.S.A. and Canada. Probably, in addition to nerve gas, the missiles will be loaded with various deadly bacterial toxins and bacteria and quite likely new viruses of even greater lethal power than the measlepox, able to attack and kill people in as short a period as twenty-four hours. We also believe that, in the temporary paralysis of cities, military posts and air bases achieved by the nerve gases, they will attempt to land airborne or rocket-borne troops to capture and hold our main centres. As you know, we are not mobilized because there isn't supposed to be a war on. Their plan might be fantastic enough to succeed."

"Who dreamed all this up?" said Pat, skeptically.

"It's no dream," the Colonel said. "There's a strong moderate element in Russia today, mainly in the Armed Forces and the new managerial classes, that is sick of dictators and war. They have contacted us and are ready to revolt when the Reds are a bit more disorganized and the people still more starved and discontented."

"Where do I come in?" I said.

"You are still a Lieutenant Colonel in the army reserve."

"That's right."

"The President himself, on the advice of his counselors, asks that you volunteer for special duty. As there is no declared state of emergency, you cannot be recalled. In fact if you don't want to leave Canada he can't force you to. He simply requests that you volunteer."

"That's all lovely, and very sweet of the old boy," I said sarcastically. "Why me?"

"On the Imjin River, in North Korea, there is a large plant which is very busy manufacturing those deadly viruses I talked about. The Russians have quietly taken over the country, and in fact the whole of China, since probably there are less than fifty million healthy Chinese alive today. The crowding into communes in the Fifties really facilitated the spread of the measlepox we hear. We think the Kremlinites want to keep an eye on them; probably want to sterilize with the S-Flu, those left by the other diseases. To have such a dangerous factory well away from their own homes and close to their enemies in Japan, as well as reasonably convenient to the submarine pens around Vladivostok, are other likely reasons for its location there. Whatever the reasons, the factory is there. Now, by good luck, the senior virologist is one of the moderates who is heartily sick of all this killing."

"Hear, hear," the Chief said. "I know exactly how he feels."

The Colonel nodded and went on. "He has agreed to give us the biochemical formulas of the viruses plus methods of growth, how to make the vaccine against them, and finally a sample of each culture to work with. We believe that if we have that information…and also we hope to sabotage their installation…we can defeat the attack before it ever starts. We plan to destroy their nerve gas centers at the same time and aid the rebellion," he concluded, "but that doesn't concern us here."

"I still don't see what I do," I said, although I had an uneasy suspicion.

"You were a paratrooper, weren't you? And you served in Korea."

"Yes, a long time ago," I admitted grudgingly.

"And you are a virologist?"

"You know that."

"You also speak some Japanese, Korean and Chinese."

"I wish I'd never admitted it."

"We want you to parachute into North Korea with a Special Forces Group, go to this plant, get the necessary information and sample viruses. The information cannot be written down for security reasons and because of this and the dangerous nature of the viruses we feel that only a man of your qualifications can be trusted to handle it."

"That's what I was afraid of," I said.

"Will you do it?"

"In the name of heaven, Colonel!" I exploded. "Twenty minutes ago all I had on my mind was catching a fish for supper and now you want a snap decision that may cost me my life."

"I'm sorry, Doctor," his face froze again, "but we haven't much time."

"The hell with deadlines," I growled. "I'm not on active duty now and no damn chairborne Pentagon pencil pusher is going to impose a time limit on me. Let him get out and do it himself if he can't wait."

"Unfortunately you are the best qualified," he said stiffly.

"Yeah, unfortunately for me," I sneered. "How is it the guys best qualified for the dirtiest jobs don't seem to be best qualified for promotion too?"

"John, please!" Pat put a hand on my shoulder.

"Sorry Colonel," I choked down my anger. "You hit some raw nerves with that best qualified remark."

"I'm sorry too, Doctor. We know you've already done more than your share. Perhaps if you think it over for a while, you'll want to help us."

"How do you propose to go about it," Hallam said to Jones.

"Colonel Macdonald, or a substitute, will have to renew his airborne training and get into first class physical shape. There will also be language school to brush up on his Korean and Japanese, with some basic Russian."

"Why Japanese?"

"It was the official language in Korea until after World War Two and many of the older people can speak it. What he misses in Korean he might be able to pick up in Japanese."

"How long will this take?" Pat said.

"About six months. Then there will be a month of special preparations for the attack itself. After that we wait for the right weather and the psychologically correct moment. The idea is to delay until the last possible moment before the Reds are ready to attack us and pull the rug out from under them. We hope the confusion and loss of morale will be so great that the partisans or maquis or whatever you want to call them will be able to rise and overthrow the communist regime."

"Adding all this up," I said, "I gather you expect the special training to start in about two weeks from now."

"That's right," Colonel Jones said. "That's why we need an answer soon."

"I have one week left of my vacation before I return to Vancouver. I'll let you know then."

"Thank you. I'll leave all the necessary information with Dr. Hallam at his office." Jones got up, bent slightly in Pat's direction and again to me, while he gave us a formal handshake. He climbed over the side and got into the amphibian without a backward glance.

"I wish I hadn't had to do this," the Chief said hurriedly as his big hands reached out for ours. "Try not to let it ruin the rest of your vacation. God bless!" He squeezed and my hand tingled until long after his great frame had vanished into the cabin of the flying boat.

After they had gone Pat cooked the fish I'd caught and we sat down to eat and talk things over. I hadn't committed myself in any way. My days as an eager beaver soldier were long gone and I was remembering the old army saying, "Never volunteer for anything." Pat had been unusually quiet. I knew she would go along with any decision I made but it is still not an easy thing for a woman to sit still while her man is thinking of committing what might turn out to be suicide.

"Want a drink?" she asked, getting out the bottles before I could answer. She mixed us a rum collins, taking the last of the ice from our little refrigerator.

"Well, what are you thinking?"

"I'm thinking just how much hell the next eight months will be."

"Hell for both of us, darling," she said. She leaned across the narrow table to kiss me. "I'm glad you want to do it. It may not win the war but you'd never be happy again if you didn't try."

I didn't relish the idea at all but I knew she was right. I'd always been a volunteer. It was too late to change. I heaved up off the bench and went on deck. The stars were out now and high overhead an Alaska-bound plane hummed by, its green and red lights winking.

"Red light...green light...GO," I thought and remembered again the quivering anticipation as I stood in the door of the C-119 watching for a little green button to flash on. I shivered with old remembered fears and I felt Pat's arms go around me from behind as she kissed the back of my neck. I think she sensed my trouble. She knew how I had sweated out jumping and the long strain of combat duty.

"Come down below, sweetheart, it's bedtime. Come and let me help you forget. There are so few nights left."

I rolled over in the soft sandy ground and pulled hard on the risers to spill the air out of my parachute. The breeze was dying. The spotted cloth wavered, flapped, and the canopy collapsed. I got to my feet, hit the box and stepped out of the slack harness. Slowly I straightened the canopy, folded it over my arms down to the backpack and tightened the straps over it. I picked the whole thing up and zipped it into the carrying bag. The trucks were waiting across the drop zone. I heaved the heavy bag up across my shoulders with the handles on each side of my neck and started towards them. My first jump was over. I was tired...tired...tired and quietly proud. The first one was past. I was a paratrooper again.

"How was the jump, Colonel?" A small black haired officer of about my own age came up behind me. Captain Balakireff, the son of White Russian refugees and lately of Shanghai, China, spoke with a faint accent. His thin lips and hollow cheeks reminded me of the ascetic saints on a Russian ikon. He should be wearing a beard, I thought.

"Pretty good, Blackie. It's been a long time."

Trudging beside him through the loose sand, a tall blond and thick chested Lithuanian Captain called Makstutis grinned down at me. "Need a hand with that pack, Doc," he said, completely unconscious of the difference in our ranks.

"No thanks Mak. I may not be in shape but I'm not that decrepit."

Closer to the trucks Lieutenant Pak On, a native born Korean imitation of Balakireff awaited us. With him was Lieutenant Kim Cho Hup, a living embodiment of the Chinese god of happiness with his round smiling face and the figure to go with it. For all his weight, the result probably of too much feasting on his Hawaiian island home, Kim was quick and tough, a veteran of the early days in Korea with the 25th Division.

These four, all war veterans and career men formed, with me, the officers' component of a Special Forces team. With us, as we assembled around the trucks were twenty-five enlisted men.

All were Orientals, a few native born, but mostly Hawaiian sons of immigrants. They too were Special Forces volunteers, qualified both as paratroopers and rangers. Each had a specialty, weapons, demolition, signal, engineer, medical, and each could take over at least one other job in an emergency. They had to be fluent in one of three languages, Korean, Japanese or Mandarin Chinese.

We jumped as a team in two sticks, led by the Slavic officers. As senior officer I acted as jumpmaster in training although in the actual attack I was to be protected rather than to command. The operations plan was simple. We were to drop in North Korea in high mountain country near our objective. The three whites would masquerade as Russian officers. We hoped to pass as inspectors or medical health officers touring the country with a North Korean Army escort. As the Russians had taken control in China and North Korea, we should be able to get by, at least for a while, considering the disorganized state of that plague-tortured peninsula. A rendezvous with the agent who had contacted the enemy virologist would be arranged. From then on it was up to us. Afterwards we were to be evacuated by submarine from a pre-designated spot on the coast.

We climbed into the trucks. As they rolled down the road back to our quarters, I pulled Pat's latest letter from my pocket and skimmed once more through its well-remembered pages. Because of the danger she was no longer working with the research project but was helping Polly on the electron microscope...Polly had heard from Harry... He was in Formosa training with the Americans and Nationalist Chinese for a landing on the Chinese mainland...he had sold them on the idea...Polly was worried of course... She was too...would I please be careful...she loved me and missed me so much...she wanted me to come home safely."

I folded the letter and put it away. I'd be coming home all right! On that I was determined. No damned disease, no stupid Communist fanatic was going to stop me!

The emphasis on pure physical conditioning changed although we continued our long marches and strenuous exercises. Now we worked constantly in Russian or Korean uniforms, used enemy equipment and talked Russian or Korean. It was hard at first but gradually I achieved a basic knowledge sufficient to deceive a casual observer.

A week before Christmas General Rawlins, the Special Forces commander, called me into his office. He came around his desk as I saluted.

"You're looking fit, Macdonald. The instructors tell me your team is progressing very nicely."

"Thank you sir."

"In view of their reports I am letting you and your men off for Christmas and New Years. Air transportation will be arranged as far as possible. Warn your men again about security regulations. See the Chief of Staff for the details." His normally stern face cracked into a smile and he stuck out his hand.

"Merry Christmas," he said.

The day following my return to Vancouver was Christmas Eve. Polly and Pat and I drove out to have dinner with Dr. Hallam in his hilltop apartment. We found him dressed in a white chef's cap and apron busily sugaring the top of a ham. In a moment the girls found aprons of their own and began to get in his way. I got busy with the brandy bottle and the eggnog.

"How's the research project coming, sir?" I asked as we sipped our drinks.

"We have a variant of the FS flu now that sterilizes only monkeys. It may be the weapon we're looking for." He paused and looked mischievously at Pat. "Did you know, by the way that the original FS virus does not cause permanent sterility in primates?"

I caught the glance and her look of dismay.

"Primates? You mean humans too?"

He nodded. I turned to Pat.

"Then you aren't sterile? You didn't tell me you had a biopsy."

This time Hallam laughed outright. "How many months have you been away soldier?"

"My God! Pat...you're pregnant!"

She came to me. "Yes darling. I am. I didn't want to tell you because I might miscarry again: but I went to Ray Thorne and he says I'm doing just fine."

"Oh baby," and I pulled her into my arms. "What a wonderful, wonderful Christmas!"

It was after dinner. We sat around the fireplace in silence. To one side the Christmas tree, with its tinsel streamers and glass ornaments, threw back a shower of sparks in answer to the flames. The coffee was finished and I savored the last drop of Drambuie slowly, letting it bite my tongue with its pungent sweetness.

"I wonder where Harry is." Polly spoke as she looked into the fire, absently twirling the liqueur glass in her fingers.

"Have you had any news?" I asked.

"I got a letter this morning," she replied and added after a pause. "They left for the Chinese mainland a week ago."

The wood crackled on the hearth and the room was silent again. I thought of the bare brown hills of China; of the squalid mud huts like those I had known in Korea; of the lice and fleas, the filth and bitter cold; of the snow that sprinkled the stunted brush and dusted the stubbled rice paddies. I thought too of the death that lingered in those dank and sweaty rooms, black holes of fear and despair.

"God help them," I said fervently and added a little prayer for myself in the days to come.

Polly began again. "He wrote the letter on the assault landing craft and sent it back with the Navy. Apparently they had not managed to perfect a vaccine before they left Formosa so the party is unprotected against the measlepox. They hope to find enough survivors on the mainland to collect antiserum, provided they can keep away from Red patrols."

"It's a shame they couldn't have waited another couple of weeks," the Chief spoke up.

"Why so?" Pat asked.

"I got news this morning that our agents in Russia have sent out more of the vaccine, stolen by the partisans, I suppose. It should be available in a day or so and some of it will be rushed out to the research teams for their protection."

"Maybe they'll send another team with vaccine after the first," Pat suggested.

"I surely do hope so," said Polly, "I'm real worried about that man."

CHAPTER TWELVE

THE ACHE of parting was still gnawing at my belly like a peptic ulcer when Blackie picked me up at the airfield in a jeep.

"My goodness, Colonel, I'm relieved to see you."

"Why? What gives? I'm on time."

"Yes sir, but the operation has been advanced, you see. We leave for Japan in the morning."

"In the morning? Oh, no!" I snorted in disgust. "Isn't that typical."

***

The week after our landing in Japan, we moved out again with full GI equipment. Our enemy clothing and arms went along in sealed wooden boxes as cargo, not to be opened again until D-day. Ostensibly, we were replacements for the Korean Military Advisory Group on our way to South Korea. We landed at Kimpo Air Base, near Seoul and then moved out by truck up the road past Uijongbu into the wooded hills south of the defense line near Kumwha. In the twelve years since I had come down that road for the last time, the mud and thatched villages had been rebuilt. Now the measlepox had ravaged, once again, the stoical population. Only a few were left, the few who perhaps had fled to the mountains and stayed there starving but afraid until the pestilence had killed and passed on. So it was back to a familiar land I came—a land of silent hills; of hardwood trees standing bare and cold above the brown earth and the dead brown leaves of the Kudzu vine; a land of little streams that thawed in the sheltered spots as the February sun rose higher in the cold dry air.

We trained over the steep hills, marching up faint trails where the woodcutters once had gone. In all that wild land there was silence—the silence of the four-footed animals who, unknown to us except by some chance meeting, watched our slow approach. The long nights shortened into March and then through April. Still we waited. Rains had come now, the spring rains, forecasting the steamy monsoon of July. In the steep valleys grass showed green and the maroon-petalled anemones had already conceived. At last the cherries were in bloom. It was time to go.

The troop-carrying converti-plane dropped vertically down on the freshly prepared landing strip shortly after dark. As soon as we were loaded it took off, wavering slightly under the hammering blast of the jet engines, and then went up, sidling over the dark trees that encircled the strip, and drifting down the valley like one of their lately fallen leaves. It swung west to go out over the Yellow Sea and then circle back into North Korea. Our rendezvous was farther to the east in the wild country close to the railway that ran up the east coast from Wonsan to Hungnam. Perhaps we could lose the radar in those steep valleys. It would have been suicide to attempt it from the east, across the Sea of Japan, right into the Siberian tiger's mouth.

An hour later we were approaching the drop zone. There would be a moon before midnight to help us make contact, but now it was dark, better for concealment but difficult for recognition of our landing area. The plane slowed, the red light came on. The pilot must have picked up the signal from our agent.

"Get ready!" I shouted. The men shifted their packs and moved their feet to get the weight distributed.

"Stand up! Hook up! Check your equipment!" One by one I called the time-honored signals, the ritual so necessary before the jump. By now the aircrew had the door open and I looked out. Even with my eyes accustomed to the darkness I could see little but the dark mass of hills below us and the rough black line where they met the horizon. Above, the stars were bright. To the east a faint paleness marked where the moon was hiding. I looked down again and now a tiny green light winked up at me. It was the drop zone and the all-clear signal. The aeroplane passed on and then came back to make its run.

"Stand in the door!" I yelled. My hand holding the static line shook slightly and my thigh muscles were tight with cold and adrenaline.

"GO." The red light had changed to green and the first men were out. Shuffling from the rear the rest followed swiftly and seemed to drop on to each other's shoulders as they went through the door. The last man went by. I stepped behind him and in the same smooth motion went on out. The rush of air twisted me and a momentary black cloud blotted the stars as the tail assembly passed over. The roar faded and I floated, weightless and almost mindless, like a baby in the womb, while my mental clock ticked the slow seconds. "Three thousand, four…" The snapping of elastic and the rush of risers behind my head stopped in a sliding jerk. I looked up. Above me a black circle swayed. It was complete; no torn canopy to worry about. Alive now, I looked around full circle. Faintly I saw two parachutes below and in front of me as I glanced back the way we had come. We were dropping quickly into a steep valley, the others at a lower level where it widened somewhat. I could see outlines of the terraced rice fields coming up to meet me. In that warm, wet air I could have made it standing. The chute collapsed without a protest. I struck the quick release and stepped out of the harness. "Pretty soft," I was thinking. "I hope the rest is like this." Where the hillside joined the terraces

I found a trail that paralleled the line of our jump. I followed it down hill.

An hour later, we were all together. The slow speed of the plane, the low jump altitude and the lightness of the wind had kept the sticks from scattering. Nobody was seriously hurt. We buried the parachutes in an overhanging bank under the Kudzu and began our march down the path. As the protected one I was now about the middle of the file. The moon was rising and the light was strong in treeless areas. We kept to the blackness of the shadows as much as possible and made a reconnaissance before crossing any open space. Our progress was slow. It must have been another hour when the line stopped advancing. A short time later a whispered message came back, "Send the Colonel up front."

When I got there, Blackie and Pak were talking Korean to a small man dressed in the ragged coat and baggy pants of a peasant. Pak introduced him.

"This is Lee Sung. He has the password and knows all about us.

I took the small limp hand Lee Sung extended. "I am Colonel Macdonald, the Doctor. What do you want us to do now?"

"I have a place where you can stay," he replied in excellent English, with an accent that seemed familiar, though blurred with lack of use. "We should go there immediately."

We followed him a short distance on the same trail and then turned up a side valley where the cultivated land rapidly rose in steps and narrowed to a point at the little stream which had watered the crops. There we found the remains of a small village. Hidden behind a row of thatched mud huts that faced the fields with eyeless walls, a narrow courtyard opened abruptly to the main house. Overhanging wooden beams and tiled roof had protected the white paper walls of the recessed front porch from the weather. It was the house of a rich farmer, rich for Korea that is, and still intact.

"This is where you stay," said Lee.

Makstutis took command. "Kim, set out your perimeter guard and get the men settled down. No lights; no smoking; no talking. I'll take a look around."

"Yes, sir," Kim moved them away. I followed Lee, Blackie and Pak onto the verandah of the house, stepping quietly on the wooden planks. Sliding aside one of the paper and wood panels, we bent our heads and entered. Crouched over a shaded flashlight, Lee traced a map laid on the grass mat floor of a small side room.

"Here's where we are now. Here's the Imjin River and the village of Songdong-ni. The virus factory is less than a mile this side of the village." He indicated the spot. "It's about twenty miles from here over the hills."

"What are the trails like?" Blackie asked.

"There's a small trail, a bit slippery in wet weather, that climbs the ridge behind this house. It joins a wagon road that runs down the next valley and then you cut over the watershed to the Imjin by another trail. That one is good in all weather."

"Is it traveled much?"

"Not now. The villages over there were wiped out by the plague. I doubt if there is anybody left."

"How do we go about contacting the Russian who's going to give us the virus?"

"He's not a Russian, Colonel, he's a Pole. His name is Anders and he is the senior virologist at the factory. He is a keen botanist and it's his custom to wander alone over the hills almost every day collecting specimens. He carries a burp gun in case he should meet bandits although there's little chance of that nowadays. However, it is a good thing to remember in approaching him that all strangers are suspect. I try to catch him on these walks of his, so it's a matter of chance and may take a day or two to arrange a meeting. In the meantime, may I suggest you and your white officers keep out of sight as much as possible. Your oriental soldiers can pretend to be living here temporarily while searching for bandit gangs."

"What about food?"

"The farmer who owned this village had a well stocked store room. You will find it at the back of the house. There is plenty of rice, root vegetables, pots of kimchi...you have eaten kimchi I presume...and other preserved foods."

"What about the measlepox, doctor?" Blackie asked.

"I doubt if the food was contaminated. Besides we had one shot of that Russian vaccine before we left. It's a small risk."

"I envy you Colonel. My only protection is to run away," Lee said wryly.

"How did people survive?" I asked.

"After they became aware of the danger some took to the hills and some small villages escaped. They kept strictly to themselves and killed anyone who attempted to force his way into their area. I have a small fishing vessel at Wongpo. I took it out to sea and stayed there by myself for several weeks."

"Then you have no family?"

"No, my father was an exile in England during the Japanese occupation. I grew up and went to college there. We came back to our ancestral home after the World War. He and my mother died very soon afterwards. The Communists let me stay, mostly because they think I am sympathetic to their viewpoint and I have made myself useful to them. An agent has no business with a family anyway," he concluded grimly.

We talked on for some time, clearing up the details of our plans. It was uncomfortably close to dawn when he left.

CHAPTER THIRTEEN

I HAD a headache—a son-of-a-bitch of a headache to put it bluntly, and my eyes felt as if some gremlin had got in behind them and was squeezing hard on the eyeballs. It had started as a mild frontal pain when I was talking to Lee and I put it down to the tension of the jump and the subsequent march to our present camp. I'd felt a little chilly too when we got here but the nights were still cold in the hills and we cooled off quickly after exercise. I was sure the aching in my back was due to the pack I had carried, about seventy-five pounds of machine gun ammunition, grenades and some medical supplies for emergencies. But it wasn't going away and I felt lousy. I was feeling damned sorry for myself as I went to sleep. Seconds later it seemed, my eyes were wide open again and throbbing.

"Damn it, this won't do!" I muttered, and unzipped the light sleeping bag we carried. "Lord, I'm hot!" I searched the aid kit shakily. Finally I located the APC's, communist version, and then decided to check my temperature. It was 40° Centigrade, right on the line. I translated that into the more familiar Fahrenheit...104°. The bar of mercury, slaty grey in the early light, shimmered and wavered as I tried to hold the thermometer still.

"Hell's teeth! What a time to get sick."

I went over the various possibilities, forcing myself to concentrate, to think as clearly as I could. It was too soon to tell. It could be malaria, or meningitis, typhoid or typhus...I'd had shots for those two. What about dengue? Or old friend influenza? My mind was wandering now. "Too soon to tell," I said, and I swallowed the APC's. "Too soon to tell...too soon to tell...to tell. tell. knell. hell. The silly rhymes echoed down long empty corridors to my ears. I knew I was burning up and getting delirious...it felt like being drunk. "Drunk? I'm not drunk...I never get drunk now...nothin' to drink, drink, drink, nothin' to drink and I'm hot. Oh God, my head! Must tell Blackie I'm sick. I have to tell Blackie. I HAVE to tell Blackie!" It was important I knew and then I couldn't remember what was important. I had to have water. I tried to stand up.

There was a murmuring somewhere nearby but I couldn't locate it. It persisted like a buzzing fly and I was annoyed. My head still hurt and my eyes ached and I ached all over and I was hot and sticky and thirsty and weak and that damned noise wouldn't go away. Wearily I decided I'd have to do something about it. I tried to lift my head but couldn't make it. I tried again and felt myself lifted. Ahead of me a face wavered and then stabilized.

"Colonel Mac, Colonel Mac, can you understand me? Colonel Mac…"

I blinked blearily at him. I squeezed gritty eyelids together and tried again. It was Sergeant Jimmy Lee, my aidman. "Lee what is it?" My mouth was dry and it was hard to talk.

"Sir, we don't know what's the matter with you. Can you tell us?"

I shook my head and it tried to fall off. Lee propped me up again.

"You've been out of your mind for three days now and running a hell of a fever. I sponged you and gave you APC's. I even gave you a shot of penicillin when we thought you were going to die." His young face screwed up with worry.

"I've still got the fever, haven't I?" I muttered weakly. "It feels like it."

Makstutis came into focus beside Lee. "It's down some, Doc, but your face was red as a tomato and your eyes are still all bloodshot. Your urine was bloody too. Now you've got little red marks, kinda like bruises, on your skin."

"Eyes all bloodshot…little red marks." Somewhere a circuit snapped shut in my head. "God Almighty! I've got Songho Fever."

"Songho Fever? What's that, Doc?"

"It's called Epidemic Hemorrhagic Fever in the States, and it hit a lot of G.I.'s around the Iron Triangle in the Korean War."

Jimmy wasn't too young to remember. He had been in on the tail end of that fight.

"You must have picked it up around Kumwha," he said. "There's nothing you can do for it is there?"

"No more than you are doing now, unless the Reds have something we don't know about." I sipped the water someone brought and lay back.

Blackie had come in when he heard I was conscious. "Lee Sung is back," he said. "Maybe he could get something from Anders, or better still, get Anders to see you."

"I couldn't walk two minutes, let alone twenty miles."

"By Golly, we'll carry you," said Blackie. "Don't you worry Colonel." I fell asleep again with his comforting hand on my shoulder.

The trek across the ridges was rough. I can't remember much of it except the feeling of falling when the improvised stretcher tipped on the steep slopes or someone lost his footing. By now, one of our sergeants, another Korean War veteran named Lim On, was ill with what appeared to be the same disease and the morale of the unit was slipping. We had jumped a week ago and as yet had accomplished nothing. In a deserted, half-collapsed farmhouse about a mile from Songdong-ni, they laid Lim and me down on piles of straw while most of the men bivouacked in small dugouts camouflaged in the woods beside the house. We waited for Lee Sung to get Anders.

He arrived the following afternoon. A tall man, he looked like a benevolent hawk, pale smooth hair, sharp nose, keen grey eyes. He stooped under the low lintel of the hovel and stood for a while in the semi-darkness of the tiny, paper-walled room until his eyes were adjusted. Then he came and dropped on one knee by my side.

"You are a very sick man, Colonel," he said slowly, in precise English.

"I think I have Hemorrhagic fever," I said.

"There is little doubt," he agreed as his hands searched my neck and armpits for swollen glands. "See, the small blood spots on your abdomen, and your eyes. And what else have you noticed?"

I gave him the story, including what Makstutis had told me about the bloody urine.

He nodded his head. "Yes, it must be so. I cannot now prevent it, but I can help you to get well." He took a syringe and a bottle of solution from the small pack he carried. "Lee Sung told me. I brought serum. Every day you must take a dose, and the other man, too. I have no doubt he will have the same disease."

It was probably some sort of concentrated convalescent serum. I never did find out; but it seemed to help. There was no more bleeding and the fever dropped. Lim improved too and, fortunately, none of the others seemed to have caught it. I was still terribly weak and somewhat depressed but I was able to get around a bit by the end of our second week in North Korea.

The days dragged along and my strength was slow to return. I read and re-read the letter I had received just before the take-off from South Korea.

"I am getting along fine," Pat had written, "in spite of feeling somewhat bloated and clumsy, which, after all, I must expect. We had some more news about Harry. Apparently the raiding party he was with got ashore all right and set up their headquarters in one of the small villages near the coast. They seem to be getting along real well so far.

"I am so glad Polly is staying with me, we are good company for each other. When I got the letter from General Rawlins that told me you had left, I was relieved in a way, as I had wondered why you didn't write. Now at least I know and I am sure you are glad that, one way or another, it will soon be over. I don't expect to hear from you again until your mission is completed. Darling, please be careful. The General told me you had had shots for the measlepox, (they sent some out for Harry's team too), so I am not quite so worried. At least the dangers you face will be those of a soldier and you will have a fighting chance."

"She obviously had never heard or had forgotten about Hemorrhagic fever," I thought ruefully, the pages trembling in my fever-weakened hands.

"Dr. Hallam is often over to see us in the evenings," she continued. "I believe he is really fond of Polly...and she of him...but naturally he doesn't express such feelings. If anything happens to Harry I'm sure he will take care of her."

"And who will take care of you and the baby if I don't come back," I thought as I crumpled the letter and burned it. We shouldn't have carried that last batch of mail into the airplane. It was the one sentimental chink in our disguise. As soon as I was well enough I checked to be sure that everyone else had destroyed all mementos. I was not naive enough to think that we could keep our secret if captured, but pages of letters could be misplaced or fragments blown away and picked up by anyone coming into the area.

The Rangers kept busy. Only one or two remained in the house to cook and look after Kim and me. The rest lay low during the day and reconnoitered by night so that they were soon familiar with the layout of the virus factory and the surrounding country. They briefed me on every trip they made until I felt I knew it almost as well as if I'd seen it myself.

That week, Anders came three times. We always had guards posted and, once he knew he was safe, he relaxed and talked quite volubly in Russian or English.

"It may be fortunate for you that you have had Songho Fever," Anders said, during one of these early talks.

"Why so?"

"The western world has not yet discovered the cause of it, but we have."

He was obviously proud of the achievements of his laboratory, in spite of the horrible use to which they had been put.

"It's a very simple virus, carried, as you suspected, by mites which live on small rodents. We have now taken that virus and changed it so that it does not require to pass through other animals as part of its life cycle. It can now pass in droplets of sputum from one man to another. In the process of change it has become much more virulent, almost one hundred percent fatal, I would say, with an incubation period of only one or two days. Also it is now extremely infectious and, I believe, far worse than the measlepox. That is the virus we have begun producing, in large quantities, in our factory."

"What are the symptoms of this new disease?" I asked.

"It acts much like the natural disease except for its extreme rapidity. There is a tremendous increase in the hemorrhagic tendency, with fatal bleeding into the gastrointestinal tract, the urinary system, or sometimes the lungs. The victims die in shock within forty-eight hours, as a rule."

"How do you know how it will act on human beings?" I said curiously although I thought I already knew the answer.

"Our people are more realistic than yours," he said, quite sincerely. "We offered men condemned to die a pardon if they lived after being exposed to the virus. Most of them agreed."

"I'm surprised they got a choice," I said acidly.

"Our rulers have softened since the days of Stalin," he replied with a wry smile.

"Why didn't you use it instead of the measlepox?" I asked him.

"We did not have enough, and also we did not have a vaccine against it until recently. In fact only a few people have been protected. I am one, and so are my helpers in the Laboratory…and, to some extent, so will you be for a while."

"Do you really think so?"

"We have found there is limited cross-immunity from having had the natural fever, especially early in convalescence, but that protection wears off rapidly."

"What do you mean by limited?"

"Let us suppose you had an accident with the vials I shall give you for your return journey and spilled the contents on you. You would be very ill with the fever but you would have a fair chance of living."

"Have you given the new syndrome a name?"

"Yes, a melodramatic one. We call it the bleeding death."

In the third week of our stay he came unexpectedly, late on a Wednesday afternoon. I talked to him alone as the other Officers had gone on an early patrol. He was extremely agitated.

"I believe the counteroffensive will soon be starting," he said. "The Americans have refused to sell any more food to us and our radio is full of reports that the return of another wet spring in Europe and drought in Siberia is their doing. Today we were ordered to load all our available virus for shipment to Russia. We expect to send it Saturday."

"How will it go?"

"In refrigerated tank cars," he replied, and seeing my amazement, he added, "We do not have a bottling plant here. There are barely enough immune technicians to load it and seal the containers properly. I have been told there is an automatic bottling plant in Siberia which can put the virus in missile warheads without human aid, but of course I am not completely informed about these things."

"God! They must be desperate if they intend to let this thing loose on America without being immunized themselves."

"A calculated risk, Colonel. We can produce vaccine rapidly and protect those who matter before the disease rebounds to our lands."

"Those who matter! That's good! I'll give you three guesses who makes the decisions."

On their return that night I called in my officers and explained the situation.

"We must stop that stuff from getting out of here," I said at the end. "In fact, if possible we should blow up the tank cars and let it all run out and at the same time try to put the laboratory out of action. It won't do much good now for us to take the virus home…there would be too little time to produce a vaccine against it even if we have the formula."

"There's a railway bridge about two miles from the plant, about four from the way we'd have to go, that crosses a deep ravine," Makstutis said. "It's on the spur line from the main Wonsan-Vladivostok railway. That's the only way out of this fever factory of theirs. We can put demolition charges on that to blow when the train goes over. There's only three or four bridge guards. I'm sure we could cut the telephone wire and handle them before the train gets there."

"Suppose not all the tank cars are destroyed," Kim said. "Could they use that crap again, or would they go near it?"

"Yes, they would," I said. "Some of the technicians are protected by immunizations."

"Then somebody has to be designated to explode the tanks in case they survive the drop," Blackie said. "And what about the train guards?"

"You're so right!" I said. "That makes me the mouse that ties the bell on the cat. You boys hold off the guards, I'll get the tank cars."

"Hell, Doc, you've lost your marbles!" Makstutis burst out in amazement. "That's our job. We've got to keep you all wrapped up like a dame in mink so you can tell them back home what's in that lousy stuff."

I laughed at his pop-eyed indignation. "That's true ordinarily, Mak," I said, "but this new virus is one hundred percent fatal if you get it. Anybody who blows those tanks is likely to get some on him, especially since they'll be damaged by the fall into the gorge. But people who've had this Hemorrhagic fever are partly protected, especially while they are in the convalescent stage, as I am, so I'll have to explode the tanks."

"I still don't like it, Colonel," Blackie said.

"Look, Blackie, if you get this new fever you die for sure...and probably all the rest of the unit will die too. Then how do I get back to the States?"

"But if you blow it, sir, we can't bring the formula home," Kim said.

"That's true, but that's the lesser of two evils. We must destroy the virus, and if possible the factory too, before they shoot the stuff over to North America. If we don't, knowing the formula will be like a condemned man knowing how he's *going to be executed*...what difference will it make?"

"Geez, Colonel, I don't know," Makstutis began.

"I do," I cut him short. "And I'm going to get those tanks. That's an order. It's certain death for anyone else."

"Except me, Colonel." Lim On stood up as tall as five feet three would stretch. We had forgotten him sleeping in the corner on a pile of straw and he had heard the last part of our argument as our rising voices awakened him. He looked about as pale as a yellow-skinned man can, which to me seems more a ghastly green, but he was steady enough, and determined enough to argue with me when I tried to set him down.

"Colonel, I'm the demolitions man of the section," he persisted. "I'm as fit as you are, and, if the Colonel will pardon me for saying so, I know a lot more about it than you do."

"OK, Sergeant," I gave in, "I'll carry the charges and you set them."

The next day Anders was back again, his bird face no longer amiable but haggard and harried. "The tank cars begin loading tomorrow morning. I believe they will go out as soon as finished, which should be shortly before sunset. The Commissar is worried about possible sabotage and, I believe, has falsified the departure time." He pondered for a moment and then looked at me. "Colonel, I am afraid to stay here. May I go with you when you leave?"

"You may," I said slowly, "if you will do something else for us. Otherwise I think it would be better if you pretend to know nothing and stay behind." I explained our plan to wreck the train and then added, "We will be concentrating on this attack and won't be able to come back and pick you up. Obviously you will not be able to go with the train after it is loaded so you could not find us. On the other hand," I paused to estimate my man, "if we were able to have help to get inside the camp and sabotage it, you could escape in the confusion and come with us."

"But what about the formulae?" he asked anxiously. "Are you not coming to get them from me?"

"We would like to have them, of course," I replied. "But it is not worth the risk for them alone since there will not be time now for our people to set up production facilities."

"You ask a lot of me," he said heatedly. "I could easily betray you and stay in the factory. You could not remain here indefinitely."

I threw a trump card. "What makes you think the factory is going to stay here indefinitely?"

His face seemed to sicken as I watched. "This means atomic warfare," he said, "and the end of the world."

"If we have to die, you are going to die too. You have about two weeks." I was exaggerating, actually it was two months. "If we don't report success to our headquarters by that time, an atomic submarine, armed with a Polaris missile with atom bomb warhead, has orders to obliterate this whole area."

"No," he shook his head. "No—this is too much. I have had enough of this killing. I will not betray you."

"I didn't think you would," I said dryly.

"But I must come with you," he said. "I am afraid the Commissar is becoming suspicious. Yesterday we were warned by intelligence to expect parachuting American raiders and the political commissar was asking me about my botanical excursions. He doesn't like me anyway because I am a Pole, and he may have put someone to watch me and report on my movements." I looked at Blackie and he raised his eyebrows. Was this a shrewd guess on the part of the Russian G-2 people or had some of our rangers been picked up?

"Poor devils," I thought. "They're probably being brainwashed right now. Time is running out on us, for sure. We must get moving right away."

Anders was saying, "What do I have to do for you?"

I told him my plan, slowly and carefully.

"One thing more," I said, as he started to go out the door. "Don't forget to bring samples of the viruses and vaccines with you...and anything else you may think important."

"I will do that," he promised. "Goodbye and good luck, Colonel."

When the sound of his steps had faded, Blackie spoke again.

"You're taking quite a chance, Colonel. He knows enough now to ruin us all."

"Yes, I am. He is a proud man and I played on his pride as a scientist. Deep down, he probably is ashamed of having prostituted his discoveries for the purpose of murder, even though there wasn't much he could have done about it. He wants to make amends and I think he will go with us. Anyway, I could see no other way of doing it, could you?"

I looked around the circle of officers squatting on the rice mat floor. "We're with you, Doc," Makstutis said. "All the way, by heaven."

Three heads nodded in agreement.

CHAPTER FOURTEEN

AT last light we sent out a small party to set up a diversionary attack behind the factory. There was a little gully screened by low bushes that seemed a suitable place from which to fire. It could not be approached in the daytime without some danger of observation. The plan here was to bury small charges on the railway line to be fired from the gully just after the train had passed. This would twist the rails and prevent the engineer from backing up to the factory again. A few well-placed rounds should help to speed him on his way down the track, and if the shots punctured some of the tanks, so much the better. After the charges were laid, two men were to be assigned to stay and do the shooting. They would rejoin us later.

Late the following morning, we broke camp. We carried only weapons, ammunition, demolition charges and one day's ration. Sammy Lee, the aidman for Blackie's section, also carried his aid kit and extra dressings. I brought mine along for our section. We moved out with extreme caution, our scouts well ahead. We could not afford discovery now, of all times. At fourteen hundred hours we stopped for rest and food. For a while I let the men relax. Then I gathered them around me except for the guards.

"We separate here," I said. "Captain Balakireff and Lieutenant Pak and his section will go to the virus factory and carry out the plan for which you have all been prepared. Captain Makstutis, Lieutenant Kim and I will lead our party to the bridge. From now on you must start thinking and acting like Koreans, at all times. You must not speak English under any circumstances. The Reds will be hunting for us after the raid as guerrillas. If they find out that we are Americans the chase will be ten times as fierce. It might even make the men in the Kremlin decide to launch an open attack on the United States. Certainly if they capture us it will give them an excuse to do so. You must not surrender. You will take no prisoners." I looked around the group and paused for effect.

"How many of you have had the S-Flu?"

To a man they raised their hands.

"Then remember that," I said, "whenever you feel soft-hearted. These are the people who did it to you."

I turned to Blackie and Pak. *"Itdah popsidah...*see you later," I said in Korean and shook hands. The two officers sprang to attention and with wide smiles on their faces gave me the communist salute. I returned it. Pak faced his men, the smile gone. A stream of rapid Korean orders poured from his thin lips. The change was amazing. What had been a bunch of slouching G.I.'s having chow in comic opera uniforms was transformed into heel clicking, jumpy NCO's barking at slightly harassed, overly anxious oriental soldiers. They quick-stepped down the trail and out of sight. A minute later we too were on our way.

Ahead of me, as I looked back towards the virus factory area, the tracks went straight over the single arch of the steel bridge that spanned the narrow ravine and, slowly dropping, twisted to my left behind a small hill to be lost about a half a mile away. I was lying in the brush on top of the hill that rose in a steep curve out of the gorge. To my immediate right, a deep cutting with jagged rocky walls slashed through the hill from where the bridge jumped the gap. Fortunately for us, the side of the ravine farthest from the virus factory, where I now lay, was much higher than the other, which enabled us to control the approaches. The rise in gradient would also slow the train. It was a marvelous trap.

We had crossed the fast-running foamy little river higher up, where it dropped down from the steep mountain ridges. Now, in the cleft below, I could hear the deeper growling as it fought for space among the heavy boulders of its bed. I was tired after the march; tired enough to quit right there. A few feet away, over the reverse slope in a little hollow, Lim On was concentrating on his demolition charges, his skeleton face immobile and thin fingers working surely as he fixed the special fuses. He had finished three, with two to go. Anders had told us there were five tank cars. We had to get them all.

I rolled over a little, the better to reach my pants pocket where I had a pair of tiny Japanese field glasses. The sun was warm and, under the special steel of the American-made Russian model helmet, my forehead was wet where the headband touched. Like all the others, I was wearing one of the new lightweight plastic body armor suits under the uniform. It was good to know that even a burp gun bullet would bruise but not penetrate. Only high velocity rifle fire could cut through the flexible weave but I wondered momentarily if it was worth all the sticky discomfort to wear it. The glasses were up to my eyes now and I waited, propped on my elbows. The round magnified world was blurred by the heat waves and the exhaustion, which blunted my concentration and sent quick tremors through my tired arms. A fly found me, his feet tickling my face as he sucked the sweat drops. The crawling became intolerable and I had to brush him off. When my eyes adjusted again to the glasses I saw Makstutis and Kim, with seven men. They were filing down the edge of the cutting in full view.

As they neared the abutment, a soldier came out of the bushes at the side of the bridge. Seeing the officers, he saluted smartly and, a moment later, called to a companion who joined the group. Then Kim and four men moved off across the bridge to where another pair of guards had come out of hiding. Thirty seconds later it was all over. At the near end of the bridge, two of my men had moved casually behind the enemy soldiers as they talked to Makstutis. Suddenly they wrapped their left arms around the victims' faces to stop a shout. Their right arms came up and the commando knives flashed down into that soft triangle behind the collarbone. It was done almost in rhythm, like some hellish ballet. The dying men writhed a little and then went limp. By the time I swung my glasses to the other end of the bridge, the scuffle there was already over. I lowered the binoculars. My stomach churned a little as it had done on my first visit to a slaughterhouse. The rest of our men were now out of hiding and working furiously on the bridge, setting up the charges. Up from below, his face covered with sweat and breathing quickly from the climb, came Makstutis. He sat down beside me.

"Dead easy, Doc," he said, as he got his breath.

"Dead, easy, is right," I said grimly. Killing of any kind always depressed me.

He glanced sideways at me, "Feel OK?"

"I'll make it," I replied quietly, with much more optimism than I felt.

We zigzagged down to the bridge. Kim was dispersing his section along the rim of the gorge and up on both sides of the cutting. We would have to eliminate any Commies who were stranded on our side by the explosion but we wanted to leave a line of retreat open for the rest. None of our men would stay on the other side. Any who survived on the far side of the ravine were welcome to go home...and I hoped they would. We settled down in the brush to the left of the bridge— Makstutis, who was to set off the charges and then go where he felt he was needed, Lim, who would be with me, and Sergeant Kang and Corporal Hip Sing who were to cover us as we blew up the remaining tank cars.

The sun was lowering to the hills now and soon would drop behind them. The waves of its heat shook the rails in the cutting, the mirage twisting them in fancy as the explosives would soon do in fact. A weak little breeze came fitfully up the tracks and cooled my face. The soft sad whistle of a locomotive drifted with it and seconds later a dull thudding noise. I thought I heard a faint crackling of rifles.

"And away we go," I said inanely.

As Blackie told me much later, the first part of the attack went off as smoothly as a Tri-Di melodrama.

"I took the men down the trail at a good pace," he said. "I wanted to get into position and take a long look at the layout in daylight. There wasn't much movement, a guard or two patrolling the fence and in the gatehouse, with my glasses, I could make out a couple of soldiers playing rummy or poker or whatever these people play. We didn't dare get out behind the plant for a look but I could hear some noises and occasionally an engine huffed and puffed like they do when they are shunting. About seventeen hundred hours a loud bell signal went off. I was frightened it might be an alarm but it must have been chow call or the end of a shift. Anyway, a few more men came out and walked about here and there and the guards changed.

"Getting close to eighteen hundred I was wondering if anything had gone wrong when I saw the guard get up and answer the phone. Maybe this was it. I alerted the men. About three minutes later I saw a tall man I thought was Anders coming down the front steps of the factory with a haversack slung over his shoulder. He moved towards the gate and we came down off the hill, going fast. By the time we got there the guards were out, watching us come, and Anders was apparently clueing in their leader.

"Why, hello, Captain Balakireff," he said as I came up. "I didn't know you were out in this part of the world. Are you the group searching for the guerillas?" I admitted we were and said to the sergeant of the guard, "Let us in. I have to report to the Commissar."

"He opened the gate and we began to enter as the train whistle blew. I was stalling for time, exchanging small talk with Anders, when the explosions came and then the shots.

"It must be the guerrillas! Behind the plant!" I yelled. "Follow me." I took off on the double with the boys coming right behind. I skidded around the corner and, by Golly, I ran smack into the Political Commissar's fat belly. Anders told me later who he was. When I got to my knees I saw he had four Russian guards with him so I guessed he must be a honcho. There was no time for argument. If I tried to play along and he found out, we were finished.

"Get them!" I shouted in Korean, and jumped on the Commissar again as he got up. Our men were fast with the knives but one guard got off a few rounds with his Tommy gun as he died. They hit poor Kwong Lin, our demolitions man...punched holes in him through his thighs and his neck where the suit didn't cover. Sammy says he couldn't do a thing for him. I didn't wait around to see.

"Hold this old fool and keep him quiet a minute. We may need him," I said to one of the boys. "The rest of you cover while Pak and I clean out the power house." I stooped down and pulled the bag of explosives from Kwong's body. Pak was away ahead of me. He was already going up the steps and hit one guy in the belly with a couple of slugs as they met in the doorway. Knives were no use now. We whizzed around inside that place like a couple of squirrels playing tag. Up and down the ladders, and everywhere we went we slapped beehive blasters with quick fuses, on generators, transformers, anything that looked important. The first ones were going off as we set the last and one of them blasted me out the door with the shock wave. I picked myself up for the second time, feeling like the last pin in a bowling alley, and looked about for my burp gun. I found it just in time to join in a nice firefight. The Reds had caught on by now. The doggoned alarm bell was making the dickens of a racket and a bunch of soldiers came charging around the corner from the railway yards. The boy with the

Commissar fired first and knocked down three and the kids covering us at the powerhouse got two more as they scrambled for cover back around the corner. We started for the gate with Benny Quong and Joe Park covering the rear. Meantime some bright so-and-so had got up on the second floor and he leaned out and dropped a grenade down between them. We got him right after the bang but it didn't do those two any good. The shrapnel went up under their helmets and caught their legs as well. I hope they died fast. Sammy wanted to go back for them but I dragged him along with me. I figured we had to get Anders out of there with the big secret and we were expendable until we did.

"By now Pak was prodding the Commissar around the corner in front of the guardhouse with a knife in his backside. We came in sight and found the four guards watching for us— Anders was standing by the door.

"Tell them to open that gate," I screamed at the fat boy. He opened his mouth but it was no use. Either somebody had it in for him or else those goons really obey orders. The alarm had gone off and the gate was closed and that was that. We kept walking. Pak stuck him again and he let out a yelp. That's when the guard commander figured the setup as fishy. He lifted his gun and sprayed. Of course all of us hit the dirt, firing, when he started to act mean, but the old Commissar wasn't a combat man. He was still on the way down when he got it in the throat and crumpled up on top of Pak. By Golly, it was a mess. Pak came up looking like a Red Indian instead of a Korean and then he blew his stack. He let out a shriek of rage like a runaway stallion and started straight for the gate, shooting from the hip. He knocked out the commander and one more and the other two beat it behind the guardhouse. Where Anders had got to I don't know. I think he went inside, but he wasn't in the guardroom when we reached it. It was getting pretty hot with rounds coming in through the windows from the three floors of the factory and some from around the corners; fortunately the gate was partly protected by the guardhouse or we'd never have made it. Pak went out and dragged the dead commander into the door to look for the gate key but a sniper got him in the arm. That was when I knew we had to get out fast or die. I sent Sammy to fix up Pak and detailed Sergeant Wong to blow the lock to pieces while the rest of the men kept the snipers' heads down with continuous fire. Then I remembered Anders. I poked my gun around the back end of the guardhouse just in time to hear a couple of shots and see the two guards go down. I hollered and he stepped out of the door of the latrine holding an automatic. I guess he'd got tired waiting and decided to finish it himself.

"Good, Doctor, very good," I said. "Now let's get out of here."

He looked a bit shaken but he tucked his haversack under his free arm and we ran for the gate.

"Well, that's about all there was to it," Blackie concluded. "We got to the woods with no more casualties and left three men to cover the open area for a while and discourage pursuit until it got dark and we could get lost. Most of us had a scratch or two and Pak was woozy from loss of blood but we got back to the old village all right and waited for your party to come in."

***

As I said before, Blackie told me all this much later. At the time they started fighting we were lying hidden in the scrub by the gorge. Makstutis had a transistor switch to the demolitions in his hand. He and I were right beside the track. We would move to safer places when the train came in sight.

"Make sure the last tank car is on the bridge before you blow it," I said anxiously. "If one is left on the far side we'll never get to it."

"OK Colonel," he said. "It's all set up. Should be a piece of cake, as the Limeys say."

Ten minutes after the first explosion we heard the quick hard slapping of the beehive charges and the rattling as the firefight got going.

"Sounds like they're having plenty of trouble," I muttered.

"Yeah, I guess so," Makstutis admitted, "but that Blackie's a hot shot and so are Pak and his boys. I'll bet they make hash outa that joint."

"They'd better or they'll be in the stew themselves," I said, in a weak attempt at levity.

He gave me an anguished frown and then, his face suddenly grim shushed for silence. Faintly I thought I heard an engine straining up the grade. Makstutis crawled over and put his head to the rail.

"It's on the way," he said. "Better take cover." He stood up and signaled the alert.

Lim and I were crouching behind a big rock outcropping halfway down into the gorge. A faint trail led from there to the bottom—perhaps a relic of the construction days when the bridge was being built. It was far enough away to be safe when the bridge blew up but from there we could reach the bottom in a hurry. My heart was hammering fast, partly from excitement and partly from weakness. My knees were wobbly and I could hear the blood rush past my ears. I tried to swallow but I was too dry. Now the train was around the bend and I could hear the slow chuff-chuff-chuff as it crawled up the track. The sound suddenly sharpened as the engine, a big American style steam cylinder, shoved its nose past the cutting and out on to the bridge, travelling at a walking pace. A movement at the other end caught my attention and, for a moment, a great tightness clamped down on my chest. Kim was standing at the edge of the cutting, calmly waving to the engine driver.

"The damn fool," I raged inside. "What in Hell is he doing?" And then I realized and almost wept in admiration and pride. Afraid that the enemy, already on the alert, would notice the lack of guards and stop in time, he was calmly risking his life, pretending to be one of them and enticing the Reds on to destruction. By now the engine was almost up to him. He waved again and moved casually up the embankment into the bush.

Behind the coal tender came a passenger coach full of soldiers, two flat cars and then the five tank cars. At the end, as the train clawed over the bridge, came two more flat cars, another guard coach and a sort of caboose. The bridge itself was exactly six car lengths from bank to bank. To be sure that all the tank cars would be caught, Makstutis had to let the first passenger coach get into the cutting on our side and the other one remain on the far approach. He threw the switch.

For a moment in time the bridge buckled upwards under the last tank car. Then, like a slow motion close-up, it started to bend downwards in a vee, moving faster and faster as the law of gravity took over. The rear tank car dropped into the vee, pulling the flat cars down with it. The crash of the explosion was rolling away down the canyon and now the screech of tearing metal sounded. The rear flat cars fell off to the side and the passenger coach behind them twisted over and wedged itself crossways between the main concrete buttresses and the far bank. By a miracle of bad luck it did not go down with the other cars and even as I turned away the guards came tumbling out of windows and doors unhurt. I looked towards our end. Three tanks had gone down with the bridge and lay twisted among the steel girders in the foaming river. Of the other two, one hung crazily over the angle between the steel and the bank. I could not see the leading tank car but I learned later it had remained upright but derailed. The couplings had broken just ahead of it, leaving the engine, the first guard car and the two flat cars free. That engineer was a smart man. Realizing that they hadn't much chance pinned down in the depths of the cutting, he pulled the throttle wide open and went for the open country as fast as the train would accelerate. With the wheels screeching and sparking on the tortured rails the engine bellowed up the grade like a charging bull trying to escape from the stockyards.

I didn't know all this. I could hear the roaring engine and the storm of firing that followed. It would be suicide to attack the tank cars in full view, I thought. Better first dispose of the three that lay in the bottom of the ravine. I nodded to Lim and we started down. It was slow work at the bottom. In places the river ran right to the edge of the cliff and we had to scramble around on the big boulders or climb up and down the rough rock face, but we made progress and eventually we stood under the shattered bridge. Down here the light was dimmer and the sound of water washing around the wreckage deadened the noise of the sporadic firing above. In midstream the rearmost tank car lay on its side, split open by the fall. The other two, though buckled, were intact. They had toppled off to the side of the bridge and now lay across the big rocks on our side of the river in the shape of a twisted Z. Lim laid down his gun and started to work. His lungs heaving in his poor sick chest, he scrambled over the rocks and then disappeared under the middle tank car. He came back up dripping wet and motioned for a demolition charge. I crawled to him and gave him one. Between gasps for breath and above the noise of the water and the echoing battle he shouted in my ear.

"I'm going to blow this one from underneath, at the lowest point above the water, so all the stuff will drain out."

I nodded in approval and he disappeared again. In a couple of minutes he was back. "We have about five minutes," he cried, his voice shaky with fatigue. "Let's get the other one."

I pulled him to his feet, where he stood shivering with cold and exhaustion, and picked up the guns and charges. We moved to the second car. This one was propped up at an angle with the low end dug into a patch of sand, easy to get at. I handed him another explosive and he jammed it against the steel, in the sand. He was about to activate the fuse when suddenly he straightened, twisted half around to face me and fell forward. The echoes of the shot ricocheted off the walls of the gorge. I estimated it came from across the water and in the same instant made a diving run for cover. I hit hard and rolled behind a small boulder as another shot hit it and whined away into the air. I was thinking fast. Some of the Reds must have been trying a sneak attack across the bottom of the gorge and had seen us at work. In spite of our uniforms it was obvious from what we were doing that we weren't friendly. I'd be marked down and shot if I tried to get back and ignite the last fuse. And there wasn't time now. I had to get out of there! The first charge might explode that full car like a can of tomato juice, spraying death in all directions. I was trying to get up the nerve to dash for safety when the shouts came from behind me. It was Makstutis, with Rang and Hip Sing. They had crawled up close to me when the fighting started.

"Doc! Doc!" Makstutis was yelling, "Get that last fuse started. We'll keep their heads down."

"Get back!" I screamed frantically. "The other tank is gonna explode. It'll cover you with virus."

"That's rough, Doc," Makstutis called back calmly, "but what's four men compared to millions. Better get cracking."

I felt ashamed, physically sick and disgusted. I had a chance and they had none—and yet, facing that death, they could still think of others while all I wanted to do was to lie there, afraid even to run. Oh, I could blame my sick mind or my weakened state. They would excuse it on those grounds and never say a word to me no matter what I did. But I knew better. Today I was beaten down while better men than I were still fighting.

I was up and running with the nausea of moral defeat rising in my guts. Quitter! The one word I feared above all...and it applied to me. Better to die now than have to live the rest of my miserable life with it. I felt a heavy blow on my back that threw me off stride. At the same time I heard the crack of a small mortar shell behind me and something sharp and stinging penetrated my right hip. They must be lobbing them across at extremely short range, trying to drop in behind the rocks and get my riflemen. A burp gun gnattered and chewed up the sand beside me as I reached the tank car but stopped abruptly as somebody blasted back. I stooped down and activated the fuse. I was halfway back across the open sandy patch when the first tanker blew up.

CHAPTER FIFTEEN

THERE was a faint smell of decay, of cold moist flesh, in the air. I shoved up from the sand and rose wearily to my feet. I looked down and saw the wet stain spreading over me from the back. My legs felt damp. I was too tired to care. The odor of the virus culture, of the bleeding death, was in my nose and mouth and I was too tired to care. I staggered past a rocky outcrop and almost fell. Sergeant Kang reached for me from cover.

"Don't touch me," I protested weakly. "The stuff's all over me."

"Some of it got us too, Doc. Better let me help you get away before the next one goes up."

We advanced cautiously up the ravine away from the bridge. The second tank car had blown and there was no pursuit. Apparently our men on the rim of the gorge had pinned down the attackers or else the horror of the bleeding death had driven them away. Now that my aching chest had eased a bit I could think again. We went around a couple of bends and the sound of firing died away.

"We've got to get this virus off, it's our only hope," I said.

"OK Doc," Makstutis was agreeable. "Whatever you say. The damn stuff stinks like a frightened polecat."

I led the way along the stream and found a chest-deep pool with a fast water flow. I walked right in, gun, helmet, jackboots and all, and thrashed around for a moment under water.

"Now you do the same," I said when I came out.

I had some soap in my pocket and Hip Sing produced another bar. With one man standing guard, we undressed and scrubbed ourselves and then our clothes and weapons as thoroughly as possible while the light faded. Numbly I noticed a large hole in my jacket and a ragged tear in the plastic suit. I shook the suit and a piece of iron two inches square fell out.

No wonder my ribs were sore and my chest ached! Makstutis saw it fall and grinned at me crookedly.

"Your lucky day, ain't it, Doc?"

"Yeah, out of the frying pan, now into the fire. Wait until tomorrow."

He shrugged. "That's the way the rocket roars."

We wrung out the water as best we could and wiped it off the guns. I felt better from the cold bath though I was weary to the crying stage. The wound in my thigh was small and not troubling me much so I let it alone.

"That should help a little," I surmised when we were dressed again. "At least it may protect the others from the disease."

We were starting to climb back up the side of the gorge when an ear-battering crash rolled up the river to meet us. Then there was silence.

I don't remember too much about that climb back up the gorge. I know I fell often and always there was a helping hand, a quiet word. We got back to the bridge in darkness and were stopped by Kim's guards. The fight was over. They had been waiting for us. Four men were dead, three in the fight for the train and Lim in the riverbed. Two more were wounded in the arm and head but could walk. One man had a broken leg. I vaguely remembered telling Kim how to splint it with poles cut from brush and giving him some morphine. I didn't like the risk of exposing any of them to the bleeding death but there wasn't much I could do about it right then except try not to touch anyone. Makstutis, the two NCO's and I, kept apart from everyone else and waited for the fever to strike. We kept going in the darkness, a darkness that became a dream world to me except for the steady support of hands at my elbows and the slow dragging of my feet as I lifted them and put them forward. Just one more step; one step more; one more step; one step more. We stopped and the hands released me. I crumpled where I stood and slept.

I woke to a pattern of shifting light and shade beyond my closed eyelids and a cool wind that blew across my face. I opened my eyes and slowly they focused on the leaves that rustled above me. The aching misery of my legs and body forced itself into my brain and carefully, deliberately, I sat up. We were in a thickly wooded valley. A tiny clearing opened from where I sat, bisected by a narrow stream. On the other side, about ten yards away, Kim and his men moved about quietly, cooking the last of their rice on a dry wood fire that gave no smoke. I stood up for a moment while specks whirled before my eyes as my blood pressure dropped. The feeling passed. I was still damnably weak but better than yesterday. I looked around for my companions in isolation and saw them squatting close to their own fire. They seemed normal. So far so good! We might have another twelve to twenty-four hours before the hemorrhagic fever started to raise hell with us. By that time, with luck, we could be holed up in our refuge. Maybe Anders would be able to help us. At the worst, as he was immune, he could take care of us and feed us.

I was still not completely aroused when Makstutis came over with a mixed mess of hot rice and kimchi in a ration can.

"Here's your bacon and eggs, Colonel," he grinned irrepressibly. The man just wouldn't give in, I thought. "How do you feel this morning?"

"Pretty good, considering," I replied.

I finished eating and walked down to the stream to splash some water on my face. Kim was there, washing up. I kept downstream from him.

"How are you feeling, sir?" he said, toweling his face with his undershirt.

"OK so far, Kim. I need a cigarette. Have you got any? No, not your packet! Just one. I'll ask again if I need it." I caught the black Russian weed he threw at me and dragged gratefully. "I didn't see much of the fighting at the bridge after Makstutis threw the switch," I said, sitting down on a boulder.

"I was down in the bottom of the gorge most of the time. Clue me in on what happened."

He squatted comfortably on his heels, oriental style, and I was momentarily amused at how quickly he had reverted from his western training.

"When the bridge fell down," he began, "the boys along the canyon rim all fired on the coach stuck in the approaches across the way. A lot of the Reds were hit getting out of it but a lot more made it and started a firefight across the canyon with us. That lasted quite a while."

"I saw the beginning of it," I said.

"I heard from Makstutis that some of them got down in the bottom and shot at you and you were hit."

"That's true, but I was hit by mortar fragments. Did he tell you that I'd never have got out if it hadn't been for him and his two men?"

"No, he didn't. He did tell me you all got splashed with that virus stuff."

"We sure did, and nobody except Anders is to come near us until we find out if we're going to get the fever or not. But what happened to you?"

"While the fight was going on back and forth across the canyon," he began again, "the engineer tried to take off with what was left of his train...it broke apart just ahead of the first tank car. He almost did it too! The two men I had posted up above, on either side of the cutting, couldn't do much as they were firing down at too steep an angle. They did manage to keep the Commies' heads inside the coach, however, and; when the train started up the grade, five of us were able to scramble up on the flat cars, leaving the other six guys to finish the fight at the bridge. Two of them were killed later on by an unlucky mortar shell burst.

"As soon as we got on the flat car I put a half a dozen burp gun pellets straight down the middle of the passenger coach and while they were wondering what to do about it, Tommy Lin sneaked up close and threw a grenade through the glass of the back door. But he didn't hold it long enough. Somebody fielded it and threw it right back before it could explode. Lucky for us he was too strong. It bounced out past the door and rolled over the side just as it went off. About that time I figured we had to stop the train or they'd take us to Vladivostok, so Tommy and little Rhee Sung boosted me up on the roof...it took both of them to do it...while the other guys gave the Reds a few rounds to keep their heads down, I hauled my two buddies up with me and we pussyfooted over the top, hoping the Commies wouldn't try to shoot up through the roof. It was steel anyway. That helped! We jumped down on the coal tender and the fireman saw us. Boy! Did he yell! He dropped that shovel and dived out the side like a frightened frog. The engineer took to the other door.

"By now the train was out of the grade and in open country, really travelling. I sent Rhee back over the top to warn the others, before the Reds got wise, and when I figured they were set I put on the emergency brake...it's a good thing I learned about engines on the pineapple plantations back in Hawaii..." he laughed. "Well, sir, that damned train just about stood on its nose and jack-knifed. I'll bet the gooks really got thrown about. Then I put her in reverse. The wheels were screeching like a drunk wahine at a hula, and slipping and sliding like crazy until they caught a hold. When she stopped and began to back up a lot of the Reds made a break for it. We got a few but most of them got away. When they saw we were going back towards the bridge a gang of those left tried to rush the cab. Tommy was waiting on the coal pile and mowed them down but a wild shot downed him when he tried to get back to me. I wanted to stop the train but he yelled at me to go on. I tied down the whistle as the signal and the other guys jumped. Then I gave her full throttle and I jumped too. Tommy stayed on. I guess he figured he was finished and he might as well take some of the Reds with him. Anyway they never got into the cab to stop the engine. It must have barreled down that grade at a hundred miles an hour. It smashed those two tank cars to glory and pushed the whole damn lot into the canyon."

"That was the big explosion I heard?"

"That was it," Kim agreed and added, "That broke up the fight. Good boy, that Tommy. He went out the right way for a soldier."

We set out for the rendezvous about midmorning. It would have been safer to wait for night but I was afraid the virus would knock us out and Kim agreed. The scouts reported no signs of life ahead so we marched in our two groups, a prudent interval of twenty-five yards between. The day was warm later on. About sixteen hundred hours I started to sweat a bit and I noticed beads of perspiration on Makstutis' forehead and a large drop forming on the end of his nose. He smiled weakly when he caught my eye.

"Guess I'm starting to get that fever, Doc," he said. "The other two guys have it too. How're you doing?"

I wasn't too bad and said so. The protection Dr. Anders said I'd get from the Songho Fever must be working. We went up on top of a steep ridge and I noticed Hip Sing was unsteady on his feet. I went over to him.

"How are you making out, boy?"

"I…" he swayed slightly and licked his lips…"I don't feel so good, sir."

"Sit down, son. Let's have a look at you."

His head was scorching hot and his cheeks flushed like an inebriated Japanese. I felt his pulse. Even after a rest it was over one hundred and forty. At a rough guess he must have been running a fever of one hundred and three degrees. I let him rest for a bit and then, with Makstutis on one side and I on the other, we stumbled on down the trail into the valley. He collapsed a couple of times before we got to the bottom and finally we were dragging him along, his arms over our shoulders, toes catching in the dust. Sergeant Kang followed reeling in semi-delirium but still carrying our weapons. Somehow he reached almost to the bottom of the slope, right behind us, and then pitched forward on his face. The guns clattered and rolled down ahead of him. His arms, outstretched as he fell, caught my legs and tripped me. I went down on one knee, Hip Sing crazily over me, while Makstutis struggled to keep his balance and pull us up again. We got Sing over to the narrow brook that tumbled along the valley floor and there Makstutis' knees buckled under him and he sat down. I was feeling rough myself, but not that rough.

"Get Hip Sing's clothes off him if you can, Mak," I said, and went back for Kang. He was still comatose so I grabbed his arms and jerked him down the slope to level ground. I couldn't drag him any more, I hadn't the strength. I got down on my knees and rolled him over to the water's edge. I stripped him to his undershirt and poured water over him with his helmet. His pulse was almost impossible to count, it was beating so fast, but it was still surprisingly strong. That fever had to be brought down before it fried his brains! No man can live long at a body temperature over 105° and I knew his must be at least that. Even if he recovered his brain could be permanently damaged by the intense heat inside his skull. I got him into the water with his head and shoulders on the bank. It was cold but there was no time for gentler measures. The exertion made the swirling come back in my head and I lay down beside him until the world came to rest again.

About five minutes later I heard gasping sounds and looked up. I had forgotten Makstutis and Hip Sing. The Mak was still fumbling with Sing's clothes but in his delirium he would forget and sit there, muttering to himself, while his fingers fluttered uselessly at the buttons. He was doing that now. The sounds were coming from Hip Sing. As I watched, he started to retch, his face was a sweaty grey-green. A great gush of dark brown blood came up and flowed away from the side of his mouth. He sank back and was still. I crawled over to feel his pulse but he was dead. Makstutis sat there and whispered. Somewhere above I heard a shout. Under the weary haze that covered my mind I knew I had to act but it was so much trouble.

"Doc...Doc..." I heard it again and looked up. Kim, watching back on the trail, had seen that we were not following. Now, heedless of the danger, he was coming to help us.

"Don't come any nearer!" I forced the words through the dry lining of my throat. He was perilously close already if this virus was transmissible through the air, as Anders claimed.

"But I can't just leave you there," he pleaded from the other side of the water.

"We'll all die if you catch it too," I croaked, and rallied my wits. "Kim, Anders may be at the farmhouse waiting for us. Get there as fast as you can. Tell him the bleeding death has got us. Maybe he can still help. And don't let anybody touch us, no matter what happens, until he gives the order." I heard no more. Forcing the last bit of strength from my aching muscles I turned back to Makstutis and pulled off his outer clothes. He lay there mumbling and rambling like a Yogi in a trance, the foam drying on his cracked lips. He was too big to roll into the water so I poured it on him from his helmet. The cold seemed to restore his sanity for a moment...his eyes opened. The whites were gone and, from the center of those bright-red bleeding spheres, the blue irises flickered as he tried to focus on me. He smiled.

"Good old Doc," he said feebly.

It was too much. I crouched there and sobbed, the aching tightness blocking my throat as I shakily poured water over him.

The light kept bobbing about in the strangest way. It couldn't be a firefly, too big. It was up high on the slope at first but soon it dropped down, wavering back and forth. I knew then it was a shaded flashlight and I heard the sliding of boots on the rocky path.

"That's close enough." The voice was strange at first and then I remembered that was how Anders sounded.

Until the darkness and rising fever stopped me I had kept pouring the water over Makstutis where he lay, unconscious and unmoving on the ground. Kang floated low and lifeless in the water like a beached log. I checked him once. His pulse was still there but slow and almost imperceptible. As the fearful heat rose within me I lay down in the stream beside him and shivered there as long as I could endure. Then I would get out again and return to my work. Finally, too sick and dizzy to do any more, I crawled to the bank and lay down on my back with my legs in the water to cool off the blood steaming inside me. Then I passed out.

The light flickered closer and waved about over my companions. It came to me and I squinted up feebly, trying to avoid the glare.

"How are they, Dr. Anders?" The voice came from the slope.

"One of them is dead…a corporal. The Russian and the Sergeant are very bad, unconscious. Dr. Macdonald is awake," Anders said and then, to me, "Do you understand me?"

"Yes, I do," I whispered.

"I am going to inject some serum." He was busy tying a tourniquet of rubber tubing above my elbow to bring out the veins. I felt the needle probing for the collapsed tissues and later the pressure as he pulled it out and stopped the bleeding. He jabbed me again in the biceps.

"You have had your antiserum and a sedative," he said, leaning close to be sure I heard. "Now you must relax and concentrate on getting well."

With that thought in my mind I went to sleep.

Three days later I was over the worst of it. I had bled again from the kidneys but fortunately the disease had not been severe enough to cause a massive internal hemorrhage that would have choked their filtering mechanism and killed me.

"How do I look?" I said to Anders that morning as he examined me where I lay, in the dappled shade of the clearing.

"Your eyes are very red, of course," he smiled, "and you have purpuric spots…what your laymen call bruising, isn't it…in the creases of your elbows and thighs, but I think you have been fortunate."

"I agree with that statement, Doctor," I said as I looked over at his other patients, lying there so quietly beside me. A horse fly lit on Kang's nose. Feebly his face twitched, trying to dislodge it. He lifted his right hand, bending the arm from the elbow. It stayed there, too weak to go farther. Anders shooed the fly. Kang's hand, poised uncertainly for a time, slowly fell back to his side. To all appearances he was lifeless.

"They're in bad shape, aren't they?" I asked.

"Yes, but they should recover. You saved their lives, you know."

"I did? How?"

"By using that cold water. When I checked them, their temperatures were very low, especially Kang. You might say you had put them into artificial hibernation. They were both in shock but with the low body temperatures reducing their metabolism during the crucial stage, I am sure they have a much better chance of returning to normal. I maintained their low temperatures with one of our new hypothermic drugs for the first two days. Now they have returned to a more normal state except that they are still asleep."

"They look more dead than asleep," I said and raised myself up to sit. Even that was an effort as my swimming head and pounding heart warned me. In a moment or two I felt better. I inched over to a tree and used it as a backrest. Soaking in the friendly warmth of the sun like a cat on a garden wall, I dozed off.

"Take this, Colonel." Anders' face was close to mine as he woke me gently and held out a bowl of warm rice. The sparse light-colored stubble on his unshaven chin stood out like the tattered wheat stalks on a dustbowl farm. Gaunt with fatigue, bleary-eyed and scruffy though he was, his red-rimmed eyes shone with a fierce determination to pull us through and cheat his former masters of at least three victims. I ate and watched as he gently spooned a thin paste of rice into the cracked and crusted mouths of his patients. As it touched their tongues, they swallowed automatically like patients under anesthesia, which, in a way, I suppose they were.

"Have you had any sleep at all?" I said, watching him.

"Not much. An hour here and there. I was afraid to sleep."

"Then why don't you sleep now while I watch. I can wake you easily if you lie down here."

"Thank you. I will do that. I am very tired."

I let him sleep six hours. The sun was low over the ridges and Kim and his men were preparing the evening meal when he awoke. Renewed vigor showed in all his actions as he moved about lighting a fire and preparing our rice gruel. This time I crawled over to help him with the patients. As we dripped the thick rice soup into those impassive faces and later washed the dry drum-tight skin stretched over bare bones, I asked about our plans.

"Yesterday," he said, "Lieutenant Pak On took a small party down to the coast, to Wongpo. They are to find Lee Sung and tell him that there will be a delay until you are well enough to travel. They also must try to get more food. It will be at least three days before they are back. I have vaccinated all your men against the bleeding death and we must wait until you are no longer infectious and I am sure they are immune before we escape. We cannot risk spreading the disease in the western democracies."

"Do you think it got spread when the tank cars were blown up?" I asked.

"It is quite possible. The concentration of virus in that river must have been very high. Unfortunately there are still villages down its course and along the Imjin where people live, and they may get it. For that reason we must move as soon as it is safe. If disease breaks out near the coast we will never be able to get a boat to take us off."

The thought worried me. Suppose Lee Sung died? Only he could make the contacts to get us away, I supposed, by small fishing boat out to sea where a submarine, or perhaps a destroyer, could pick us up outside the territorial limits. We had to avoid the coastal patrols too and only Sung could help us there.

By the end of that week, May was two thirds gone and we were all recovering slowly. Pak came back and the news was bad. Lee Sung and Blackie had come with him. I met them as I strolled along the trail and went back with them to our camp for a conference. Before it began, Anders got out his syringe and inoculated Lee Sung.

"We can't afford to lose our only contact with freedom," he said.

"I appreciate your kindness, even if it is somewhat self-centered," Lee replied, with a disarming smile.

"Let's have it," I said to Pak when all the officers were gathered in the glade. Makstutis, too weak as yet to participate actively, was lying quietly taking in all that was said.

"We got into Wongpo without too much trouble," he began. "We kept away from any signs of people on the way. It wasn't too hard to locate Lee Sung either when I walked into the little town; several people knew him and I pretended the North Korean Army had business with him. I found him down at the wharf where his boat is moored and he took me aboard. I was alone of course," he said, as an afterthought. "The men stayed back in the hills."

"Is that the boat you mentioned when we first met?" I interrupted to ask Lee.

"Yes. Actually it belongs to the United States," Lee Sung said. "It is fitted as a deep sea fishing or trading junk. It has souped up engines that look ordinary and a false bottom where I hide guns or radio or anything we need to smuggle into or out of North Korea. The boat is registered in my name of course. I'm supposed to be a part-time fisherman and local cargo carrier, as well as a merchant. I have a small store in Wongpo. The

Reds used to wink their eyes at my activities because I smuggled things they wanted from Hong Kong or South Korea."

"Sorry to interrupt," I said to Pak. "I wanted to get the background straight."

"That's all right, sir," he replied. "Now, where was I?"

"You'd got to Lee's boat," I said.

"Oh yes. We had to get some food so that's the first thing we talked about. Lee had bags of rice in his store so we went there and loaded up a mule cart he borrowed. We were going to drive it as far as we could to where our men could get the rice and pack the sacks on A-frames back over the trail to the farmhouse. We thought it would be less noticeable if we did it that night. In the meantime Lee went out to get some vegetables and see if he could scrounge any meat. That's when the trouble started." He turned to Lee Sung. "Maybe you'd better tell the rest of it."

"I went to the house of a farmer, an old friend of mine, who lives on the edge of the village, to bargain for some vegetables and perhaps a pig," Lee said. "I was still there, drinking tea to conclude the transaction, as is our custom, when a detachment of about fifty North Korean soldiers in three trucks rolled along the coast road into the village. I finished my business as rapidly as possible, and, with the help of the farmers' sons, brought the food down to my store. Then I walked out around the village seeking information. Lieutenant Pak stayed with the supplies. I was afraid someone would have told the detachment commander of the presence of another North Korean officer but fortunately he was so busy and the people so frightened that no one remembered Lieutenant Pak.

"That evening the commander called an open meeting in the village and announced there was to be curfew for everyone beginning that night. Anyone who disobeyed would be shot. He also announced that nobody could enter or leave the village by land or sea and he has seized the fishing vessels, including mine."

"Oh, my God!" I said. "Why did he do that?"

"Apparently a new epidemic of some sort has broken out at several villages along the Imjin River."

I looked across at Anders and shook my head. He lifted his shoulders in a shrug of resignation.

Lee Sung continued. "There is a great search being made for American bandits of oriental descent masquerading as soldiers of the Peoples Army who attacked the virus factory. You will be interested to know that it was a large and heavily armed force of capitalist reactionaries which was driven off with very heavy losses.

"Losses to whom?" Blackie asked with a grin.

"To the Americans of course. The virus factory was not damaged."

"At least that's the truth; we got the powerhouse," Pak laughed.

"The moment he made the announcement about American soldiers I left the meeting quietly and went back to my store. Somebody was going to wake up, perhaps soon. I told Pak and we decided to risk it as the soldiers were still moving into the police barracks and getting set up. We drove the mule cart quickly out the back end of the village and got away without being challenged. In fact we didn't see anyone at all until we met our own people."

"It looks like we've stirred up the whole country," I said. "They certainly seem frightened."

"I'm not surprised," Anders broke in. "When I left the factory, besides the virus cultures, my rucksack was full of bottles of vaccine against the bleeding death and as much of the anti-serum as I could carry. I expected we might need it. I destroyed all I could of what I had to leave behind and the papers too. The Communists have very little left."

"A fine piece of work, Doctor," I said. "You saved our lives and deprived the Reds of their protection, all at the same time." I turned back to Lee Sung. "I wonder how they figured we were Americans. All our papers were in order. There wasn't a thing to show we weren't native guerrillas, admittedly in the service of an unfriendly power. Why not think we were from South Korea?"

"Possibly some of the men we left in the factory lived long enough to talk," Blackie said, "but I doubt it very much. Of course seeing the white officers would give them grounds for suspicion."

"Suspicion, yes, but not fact," I said.

"The radio has been talking mysterious explosions and guerrilla warfare in Siberia and parts of China recently," Lee Sung reported.

"That's it, by Golly!" Blackie burst out. "The raids on the nerve gas centers must have started. It could be somebody has been captured and brainwashed."

"Could be," I said, "and if so, we'd better get home. If the Reds can suppress news of how successful the raids are, they may still bluff the democracies, with threats of nerve gas and CBR warfare, into giving them more food and a good settlement of the war, but if we get home with our story then they'll realize they are licked and maybe quit."

The following day we set out to do the last few miles to the farmhouse. The Reds didn't have enough men to search the hills and the wilder the area the safer we'd be. Our trouble would be to break through the barrier at the coast. With one wounded man and two sick ones on litters we were heavily loaded and could make only slow time. I had all I could do to carry my own weight and when we got to the house late that night I collapsed on a pile of straw and stayed there for the whole of the next day.

CHAPTER SIXTEEN

WE STAYED in the village for three weeks. Each day Makstutis and Kang were a little better.

"We have to get out of here," I said to Anders one day in the last week, after we had examined our patients. "The A-bomb carrier is probably on its way right now."

"They can't march all the way to the coast," Anders said dubiously. "If we must go, we shall have to carry them."

Blackie and Kim had been watching us with interest. Now Kim spoke up.

"We've got some real husky boys in the unit, Doc. How about fixing up seats on a couple of A-frames. Then we could *chogi* them up the hills and they could maybe make it down the other side."

"It's a good idea, sir," Blackie agreed. "Those back trails are too narrow for litters. We can change *chogi* bearers frequently."

"What about Yip Kee?" Kim said. "Can he travel the same way?"

I looked at Anders. "What do you say, Doctor? It's a month since his leg was fractured. I think we could take a chance on it provided he is carried all the way."

"I see no alternative," Anders agreed.

We borrowed the A-frames from the farmhouse and Pak wove basket seats across the carrying prongs. With wider shoulder straps and some padding our men could carry the patients quite well, changing frequently. We assigned two bearers to each A-frame; it was all we could spare. The first time we tried it, Makstutis, irrepressible as ever, cracked, "This'll be the first time I ever went into action sitting on my ass. I feel like a damn tanker." The name stuck; from then on they were called the tank section.

In the first part of June, Lieutenant Pak and Lee Sung made a reconnaissance and came back with an encouraging report. The furor over the raid on the virus factory had died down. Work on the powerhouse had started but in a half-hearted fashion, either from a sense of defeat or perhaps a shortage of supplies and workmen. The bleeding death had hit hard along the Imjin and spread over the watershed to the coastal villages. It continued to spread as the panic-stricken natives, completely out of control after two terrible epidemics, fled from the disease and disseminated it wherever they went. Most of the enemy troops were being used to try to halt the crazy rush away from the death zone but some of them had also become infected, either by contact with refugees or perhaps in the age-old fashion by consorting with prostitutes in the towns. The result was disorganization and a very low morale.

The garrison at Wongpo, still kept at fifty men, was in good health as they had commandeered plentiful food supplies and driven out or killed most of the villagers who had not already died. They held the harbor and the three boats tied up there. One was Lee Sung's, the other two were much smaller fishing boats.

Counting Anders and the three convalescents, we were down to a total strength of twenty-three. It would not be easy to capture the boat unless we could catch the North Koreans by surprise, but we had to try it. We set off over the wildest part of the country, avoiding all villages or farmland that might still be inhabited. By the evening of the third day we lay on a ridge overlooking Wongpo. Shortly after dark, Lee Sung and Pak went down to see what the situation was. The day had been warm but a cool breeze began blowing towards the sea as the land cooled off. I fell asleep, lulled by the quiet murmur of the distant breakers and the rustle of leaves in the steady wind.

"Doc, Doc, wake up! Wake up, Doc," the insistent whisperer was Kim.

"Yeah, what, what's that?" I struggled confusedly back to consciousness. Obviously something was wrong the way Kim was still shaking me. "OK Kim…layoff…I'm awake," I said crossly. I was still fagged out and hated to come back to reality.

"Sorry sir, there's trouble. Lee Sung has been captured."

"Captured!" I echoed. "How do you know?"

"Pak just came back. He says Lee Sung left him hidden near his store while he tried to sneak back on board the junk. He could see Lee go aboard but he never came on deck again. A few minutes later a North Korean soldier came off the boat and went to the police barracks. Two officers came back with him and went aboard. Then Pak figured he'd need help and high-tailed it up here."

"OK, get everybody up. We move out right now," I growled and started to put my equipment on. "Where's Blackie?"

"Talking to Pak, Colonel," he said as he moved away.

While the men got ready, the officers gathered around me.

"What's the plan, sir?" Blackie said.

"I'm not absolutely sure," I said, "but I do know this, if we don't rescue Lee Sung and his junk you might as well figure on walking back to the States via Siberia." I thought over the plan of the village for a moment. "The boat is lying alongside the jetty about five hundred yards north of the police barracks. The houses there thin out along the coast road. You, Blackie, take four men. Swing north from here and come in at the jetty as quietly as you can. If it isn't well guarded maybe you can get aboard before they suspect. Then wait for us. Better take Pak with you…he knows exactly where the boat is in this darkness. Kim, you take five men and surround the police barrack as well as you can. At least try to cover the way north to the boat. Don't do a thing unless you hit trouble or Blackie gets into a fight." I paused, there was some detail I wanted to be sure of. "Oh yes, locate all power and telephone lines you can and cut them the moment shooting starts. Then hold off the Commies as long as possible and withdraw towards the junk. I'll take the tank section and Dr. Anders. We'll go along with Kim as far as seems safe and then make for the boat by way of the beach while he tackles the barracks. The challenge is Pusan…the answer, Tokyo. One thing more. I don't want to leave without Lee Sung for two reasons. One, we owe our lives to him, and two, without him we'll have one hell of a time running that boat and contacting help. I'm betting he is still held on the junk but there's no guarantee of that. I wouldn't be a damn bit surprised if the Reds were holding him for bait to catch us, so watch yourselves every minute. Is that clear?"

It was. Blackie and his boys moved off first, going north over a trail that would gradually lead them down the slope and north of the village. A few minutes later we followed. Makstutis and Kang were to walk downhill although they were exhausted from the day's march, but Yip Kee had to ride. There was not quite a half moon, enough to see the trail but not enough to make us conspicuous. I looked down to the village. There were no lights. Even in the police barracks there was blackout, either in fear of guerrilla sniping or perhaps waiting for us. In thirty minutes we were on level ground with the beach a quarter of a mile away. There was little wind now and the waves must have been small. I couldn't hear anything but my own breathing and the scuffling of our feet. There were no dogs and I wondered if there ever had been; dog is a tasty meal to some of these people. Tonight certainly it was a blessing.

Kim came back to me quietly, a short strong silhouette against the low moon, and stuck his mouth up close to my ear.

"We go straight from here, Doc. The Police barracks is on the coast road dead ahead. You'd better cut north a bit before you get on the beach. Watch it crossing that road. In this light you'll stand out like a neon sign."

I nodded to him. He and his men moved away, shadows that merely faded until I was not sure they were there at all. I waited a little longer, then I took the lead with Anders next, followed by the three tanks, all the patients now riding, and the three spare men acting as a bodyguard. We walked in a wide arc, going north and finally swinging down a narrow mud lane between thatched houses to come to the coast road. In the moonlight I could see no sign of life, so, one at a time, we skimmed across it as quietly as we could, dodged the fishing net racks that cluttered the soft sand and got out on the tidal area of the beach. I saw at once that I had made a mistake. Kim was right. We were far too conspicuous out there on the hard sand. I led them back close to the nets and we stumbled on, tripping over the rocks and loose stones that thrust up through the sandy patches, tiring ourselves out in that loose shifting footing.

I stopped, trying to breathe silently. Faintly ahead I saw the outlines of the jetty, the masts of the three boats silhouetted above it.

"Let's get back beside the road," I whispered to Anders. "We have to get on it soon anyway, to approach that pier where the boats are. The *chogi* bearers are about all in, trying to carry the patients in this soft sand."

We had just stumbled and crawled back over the rocks and debris to the side of the road when a light machine gun chittered angrily to the south. I heard the yelling of commands cut short by the quick blasting crack of a hand grenade. For a moment the flame burned a pattern on my retina so I couldn't see clearly. I thought there were figures moving down that way but I wasn't sure. Ahead, where the masts of the junks jousted at the stars, there was a flash of light as a door opened. A man's harsh scream followed it as thunder follows lightning and then there was a splash, shouts, and running feet on the planks of the wharf. The firing at the police barracks was heavier now and I could see rifle flashes that appeared to come from a second floor window. One of our boys must have marked it down too. The rifle cracked once more, followed instantly by a grenade explosion inside the room. It lit up the outline of the window like a furnace door opened in a dark cellar. Something fell out. After that there was a lull behind us. Ahead, sporadic shooting rattled back and forth from boat to jetty to shore, the flashes jerking about like fireflies playing tag.

I could make no sense out of that battle so I gave orders in a low voice.

"Let's stay here right now. Tanks, dismount and cover the rear. Anders, you and the three guards move north twenty-five yards and cover both sides of the road. Stay hidden, halt everybody, and don't forget to give the challenge before you shoot." I returned to Makstutis. "I'll drop back south a bit," I said, "and outflank anybody you stop."

I walked away and hid behind poles supporting one end of a large fishing net that was hung on the long racks to dry. The shadows broke my silhouette but I could see well through the net.

Across the road the low thatched roofs of the houses formed an almost unbroken bar of shadow against the faint light of the moon. I had been looking at it for a long time. I stared at it once more and thought I saw slight movements in the blackness. I looked away and tried the old trick of not staring straight at where I wanted to see, to give my night vision a better chance. There it was again!

"Halt!" Makstutis gave the order in Korean. There was neither movement nor sound now.

"Pusan!" He hissed the word explosively. Still no answer!

The light from his grenade was an instant before the roar. Crouched along the walls of the houses across from me was a group of men, more than five, maybe ten, spread apart for safety. He had caught the first two with the explosion, the grenade right between them. The others opened up, firing generally north and across the road, hoping to catch their assailant.

"Makstutis is smart," I was thinking. "I'd probably have used my gun and given my position away first thing." I marked the approximate area of the flashes and, from my knees, covered it with one swinging burst and then dropped behind the poles. The answering fire went over my head and now our tanks really let go, all six of the men blasting at the black shadow. It was enough. There was no answer. Except for an occasional moan and some dragging and scrabbling in the dirt, I heard only the ringing in my ears. Five minutes later I decided it was safe to go back to my men.

The battle south of us stuttered and chattered as the burp guns spat at each other. Northward it was quiet, too much so. An hour went by. Then I heard the challenge again.

"Halt! Pusan!" …"Tokyo!" came the answer. It was Kim.

"What the Hell's going on?" he asked.

"I don't know," I said. "I think Blackie has the bear by the tail and can't let go. There hasn't been a sound for a long time."

"We've got the Reds bottled up in the barracks," Kim said cheerfully. "All except a patrol of ten that got out and went north. I figured you could hold them while we took care of the rest."

"We cleaned them up. They're lying over there across the road."

"That's real neat work, Doc." I imagined him smiling in the dim light. "Now what do we do?"

"Damned if I know," I admitted. "We'd better try to find Blackie, I guess."

We found him lying behind the heavy timbers of the jetty where it joined the road. He was boiling over with anger and frustration.

"The so-and-so's went back down inside the boat when the fighting started and I don't dare go after them. They've still got Lee Sung there and threaten to kill him if we attack. I told them we'd show them real torture if they hurt him and promised to let them go free if they surrendered but I guess they're counting on being rescued."

"Any of your men ever do any sailing?" I asked.

"I have a couple who know how," said Kim. "What's in your mind?"

"We can't get to the engines of the junk and I'm afraid to stay here." I turned to Kim. "Did you ever get those power and phone lines, by the way?"

"Yeah, I got them; but they could call for help if they have a battery-powered transmitter."

"That's what's worrying me," I said. "The only alternative I can think of is to get on that junk and try to sail the damn thing away. Maybe, when they find out they are at sea, the gooks will surrender. Kim, you go back and hold the fort while we try to get on the boat."

"But sir," Blackie spoke up, "when we go we'll have to take all three boats or the garrison might take after us."

"I forgot about that, Blackie," I said ruefully, and then, as the thought struck me, "Say, maybe one of them has an auxiliary motor and we could tow the whole lot out to sea. Is there anyone on the little boats?"

"I don't think so. I watched for a while when the fight started and didn't see anybody. But they're small," he concluded doubtfully. "I wouldn't bet on any engines."

"Engines or no engines," I decided, "we take all three boats. Can you get aboard them safely?"

"We'll have to rush the big one," Blackie replied. "There's a couple of ports they can fire through that cover most of the wharf except out towards the bow."

"Let's see if we can find a rowboat first, or make a raft from those fish racks," I said. "Then you can row out to the end of the wharf with three or four men and approach the junk head on. While you're about it, check the fishing boats for engines but don't start them up if they have any. Tie all three boats together and find something we can use for paddles or oars too. We'll try to float away with the tide. It seems to be going out now."

Down by the nets we found a long flat-bottomed rowboat that seemed serviceable. It was a struggle to get it to the water but we managed with the help of some choice swearing and rude remarks about Korean fishermen and Marine operations in general. The long sweep oars were stacked by the nets and, in a short time, Blackie and his amateur crew splashed out into the darkness. Some time later he was back with one man.

"We got aboard," he related proudly, "and found the two fishing boats have small motors that might be enough to pull the big junk along for a while. We've got them all tied together and I left three men on the deck of Lee Sung's boat. They can make sure the gooks keep their heads inside but we'll have to ferry everybody out to the small boats first. We still can't risk crossing that wharf."

"OK," I agreed. "Start ferrying the tanks. I'll go and get Kim and his gang."

There was no more firing around the barracks. Either the Reds were waiting for daylight or perhaps for help. The moon had set and in the blackness finally I found Kim and explained the situation. We sent off all the men and together we sat and watched for a surprise sortie from the building. It must have been about two in the morning when Blackie sent back for us. We were the last to leave and, as I passed the racks, I pulled off a fishing net.

"Give me a hand with this, Blackie, I want to take it along with me."

"What on earth for, Colonel?"

"We can't get below decks on the junk. Our food is low. We can try for fish with this. What about water?"

"Everybody filled their canteens with water before starting."

"It's not enough," I complained, "but we can't wait now."

By this time half our men were on the deck of the junk. The sick men stayed in the smaller craft in case of trouble. We filled the rowboat with six of the strongest men and cut loose from shore. With the ebbing tide to help, the rowboat crew pulled slowly away from the wharf, aided by others paddling in the fishing craft. Our prisoners made no noise and we could hear no sounds of pursuit. An hour later we started the small boats' motors.

My first impulse had been to run for the open sea, beyond the territorial limits of North Korea but I reconsidered. The Soviets, if they were looking for us, wouldn't bother about the niceties of international law. We were fair game until picked up. So we putted along the coast, running towards the thirty-eighth parallel. Shortly before dawn we sailed close in to the rugged shoreline and anchored. We loosed the small boats and ran them in to shore behind a rocky headland. Perhaps a recon- naissance plane would miss us in the shelter of the cliffs. We would have to chance the wind and weather in our rather insecure hideout.

Sitting on the pebbly beach beside Anders, I was wondering what to do next when he broke the silence.

"I believe I have a solution, Doctor," he said in his precise manner, "if you will give me permission to try!"

"What can we lose?" I said.

Approaching Lee Sung's vessel from dead ahead, we climbed over the bow. Anders leaned over the side and yelled in fluent Korean for the senior officer of the Communist soldiers. After a short silence there was a rough shout from the forward port.

"What do you want with me?"

Anders talked slowly and clearly. "I am Dr. Anders from the virus factory. You know I escaped and that I cannot go back if I want to live. Therefore, if this boat is found by your comrades I will kill you before I die myself."

"You cannot touch us and you cannot sink the boat. Your threat does not scare me." The Red officer did not attempt to conceal his scorn.

"I promise you that if you free Lee Sung we will set you ashore and let you go unharmed."

"I do not trust traitors," yelled the Korean. "We will not surrender. You will be caught soon by our patrols."

"That will do you no good," countered Anders. "Listen to me! I have vials of the bleeding death with me. All of us, including your prisoner, are protected against it. If you do not surrender now I will break the vials and spread the disease through the ship. Even if you are rescued you will still die."

We could hear the angry arguments below deck. All of them had seen death from hemorrhagic disease in its new virulent form. It was a horrible sight even to a physician, and, to the uneducated soldiers, the thought of those purple mottled bodies with blood red eyes, retching and vomiting their lives away, must have been terrifying. The wrangling stopped and the senior officer called out.

"How do you plan to do this if we consent?"

"How many men have you?" Anders asked.

"We are twelve altogether."

"Then send up four men, including the other officer, unarmed. We will put them ashore where you can see them. The second time four more will go. The last time, you will come up and bring Lee Sung. If he is in reasonable condition you too will go. Otherwise you die."

"It is agreed. We come now."

There was no further trouble.

Lee Sung had been beaten in the usual Korean fashion but he was so glad to be free he claimed he felt fine. The North Koreans disappeared quickly along the beach as if afraid we might shoot.

"We'd better get out of here right now," said Lee Sung. "They can reach a good sized village north of here in an hour and give the alarm."

"All right," I agreed. "You take over."

He led us below and, after shifting some cargo, opened up a small space under the false deck, forward of the engine room. In it he had a powerful radio transmitter, a case containing two heavy machine guns with ammunition, and a few boxes of burp guns and grenades.

"I used to run guns to the guerrillas," he explained. "These may be very useful."

We set up the machine guns on deck and I felt better. By now we were running south at the full speed of the powerful engines, the two small junks towing behind, still manned and helping with their own engines. Sung had said we might need them when I suggested sinking them before we hauled up our anchor. I steered the course while he worked his radio, trying to raise his contacts and get help to us. It took some time but finally he came on deck smiling.

"I got them," he said. "We rendezvous with a destroyer off the coast tonight. It will escort us to Japan."

"What do we do in the meantime?"

"There is danger that the Communists picked up my signals and got a bearing. If the coast patrol or the jets don't see us we will be OK."

"What about our own jets? Can't we get fighter cover?"

"Only as a last resort…and it would probably be too late. The Air Force has been warned to avoid all incidents and they do not wish to fly close to the coast."

The sun was almost gone behind the hills of the steep Korean coast when the Red jets found us. They came out of the sun, as experienced fighters do, and the high whistle was already over us before we saw them.

"Migs!" I yelled and ran to the stern. "Cut loose! Spread out and head in to shore."

The little boats swung to starboard almost at once and wavered off like water beetles trying to dodge a dragonfly. Lee Sung was at the wheel again. He spun it sharply and the bow swung towards the shore. There was shelter in a narrow cleft between a rocky pinnacle and the cliffs of the mainland if we could reach it. We would have to chance the depth of the water. By now the jets were around again and peeling off for the attack. They were coming in low from the northwest this time as we were getting some protection from the shoreline. I watched them come, feeling helpless without a weapon, ready to drop behind the mainmast when I saw the angle of flight. At the stern, Makstutis was lying flat, his helmet back on his head and his teeth bared as he squinted over the barrel of the heavy machine gun into the bright light. Beside him Kang was feeding the belts. Propped up against the side, Yip Kee braced his automatic rifle on the wooden rail and waited calmly. I swiveled around. Blackie and two others had the forward gun aimed and waiting. In the little junks, dropping rapidly astern, I saw that Kim and his men were already fighting. Their puny burp guns popped bravely at the two jets which, ignoring them as too small, were concentrating all their attention on us.

The leading jet grew larger, filling the sky with its round open face and stubby wings. The tracers from Makstutis' gun floated lazily upwards and then seemed to snap past, below the airplane, and wink out. Too low, I thought, and dropped flat as the Mig hit out at us. The ship heeled over, sliding like a runner for base as Sung clawed at the wheel. The screaming roar of the jet and the impact of cannon shells and bullets on wood went by me once, and then again as the second Mig swept overhead. I looked back. Makstutis was unhurt but Kang was rolling around clutching at his legs. I got up and ran to him. That last minute swerve and the sight of the tracers coming up had been enough to divert the pilot's aim. Perhaps the bumpy air currents of the cliffs helped. I thanked God as I ran that there were none of the new guided missile planes around. The shells had ploughed through the stern rail and ripped up the port side of the deck, missing the machine gun but catching Kang's legs.

I was down on my knees beside him for ten seconds. Probably fractures of both tibiae I estimated. No time for splints! I grabbed him by the collar and dragged him, moaning with pain, into the companionway where Anders had stuck up his head.

"Compound fractures, both legs," I screamed hoarsely. "Get him below and fix him up. They're coming back."

He scrambled up to the deck, picked up Kang with the broken legs dangling and staggered down the steps. I turned to go out but the roaring chattering horror was back. I dropped and slid down the stairs, careless of the bruises, the violent swerving of the boat throwing me off the companionway to the deck below.

I got back on deck. Makstutis was still at his gun with Yip Kee feeding the belts to him. The forward crew had been hit. Two lay quietly, limbs sprawled out in a grotesque swastika. The third man, dripping blood from one arm, was trying desperately to lift the overturned gun. In the wheelhouse the windows had been shot out but, as I ran forward, I could see Lee Sung, his face bloodied by flying splinters, hunched gamely as he spun the wheel and sideslipped and twisted desperately for shelter. I reached the fallen machine gun and propped it up, the muzzle pointing high. The wounded man was Don Lim, younger brother of the man who had died in the gorge. My throat filled up tight. Blackie was dead!

"Can you feed the belts Don?" I gasped. He nodded and his bloody hands groped painfully for them, laying them flat. There was still a little time. I dragged the bodies of the dead men in front of the gun and piled the heavy fishing net I'd brought on top of them. Blackie wouldn't have minded, I thought…and it might help some. I dropped down beside him.

We were close in to shore now and the Migs had to come in straight over us from the north. They were very low, trying to get a longer time on the target. I pointed the barrel of the gun straight back towards them and canted it up as high as it would go. There was little hope of aiming at that speed. I ducked low behind the barrier. The roar of the first Mig deafened me as I held the bucking gun, my head almost flat on the deck. Something hit my helmet hard, the jerk knocking it back off my forehead and wrenching my neck. Vaguely I felt a ripping at my left heel and a burning of the flesh. The first roar was gone and then the second. I rolled over. There, shrinking to a toy behind us, the leading Mig was climbing steeply, smoke pouring from it as it tried to gain height. It slowed, stalled, and began to nose over. I saw the pilot bail out, the ejection seat shooting him away from the plane. He dropped and the parachute opened as the Mig, twisting and gliding out of control, smashed into the hillside.

I started to get up, howling with excitement, until I saw Lim slowly fall over beside me on to the smoking fish net. He had fainted from loss of blood, his arm almost amputated by that first wound. Only as I dragged him away from the net did I realize that it had stopped an incendiary shell and saved us both. I took off his belt and tightened it around the arm as a tourniquet. Before I left him I checked, but aside from wood splinters off the deck he seemed to have no other injuries. Back at the stern I could see Anders working over Makstutis. He had fragments through his right arm but was still ready to fight. Yip Kee was exhausted and lame from his efforts but unhurt. I stood up to look for the other Mig. We were very close to shore now. Suddenly the junk lurched, scraped forward and stopped, throwing me against the rail. I pulled myself up again and looked around. We were grounded solidly between the rocky spur and the cliff. At least the Mig couldn't get at us now.

It didn't try. We heard it circle over the fallen parachute and then fly north. Lee Sung came back from the wheelhouse.

"We'll have to get out of here before a patrol boat finds us," he said. "It will be dark in half an hour. We can go in the small boats to find the destroyer."

The light was dim as we lowered the last wounded man into the small junks. We had smashed the radio after sending a final signal and then Lee Sung, his face impassive in the torchlight, placed a demolition charge on the engines and several more along the hull. I took a last look at Blackie and his buddy where we had laid them below decks. We pulled away, the engines chugging steadily. I looked at Makstutis and his face was wet. I was having a hard time myself.

In the afterglow the junk faded into the background as we drove straight away from the coast into a choppy sea, raised by the freshening wind. A momentary flash and a series of dull heavy thuds marked her end. I bent over Makstutis to adjust the bandage on his arm. He peered up at me.

"Doc, you've got holes in the head," he said and grinned.

I pulled off my helmet and looked at the neat bullet marks through the top. "Didn't let any sense in." I rubbed my sore scalp. It was only then I remembered my torn heel. I pulled off my boot and looked at it. It was only a small flesh wound.

"You and Achilles," Anders said and smiled.

"Yes, but he lost the fight. We've won."

CHAPTER SEVENTEEN

FASTEN your seat belts." The light flashed on in the passenger cabin of the Canadian Pacific Airlines jet. We were going down through the overcast. Vancouver was ten minutes away.

"Did you enjoy your flight, Colonel?" the stewardess asked me as she came by for a last minute check.

I smiled up at her. "The best part comes in ten minutes," I said, "but it certainly has been fast."

Ten days previously we had been lifted out of the fishing boats by the crew of a U.S. Navy destroyer and taken to Okinawa. The casualties were admitted to the Army hospital for treatment and the rest of us, also at the hospital for observation, were given baths, clean uniforms and a meal. Everywhere we went we were kept under isolation precautions and we were guarded as carefully as a basket of over-ripe eggs that might break momentarily.

A week in isolation convinced the officials that we were free of the bleeding death. By that time too, we had been drained of our information.

"When can I go home?" I asked, the day we were informed of our release. "I've got a wife due to have a baby anytime. I'd like some emergency leave."

That night they put me on a Military Air Transportation Service flight out of Kadena Air Force Base to Japan where I picked up a seat on the CPA flight recently resumed for military purposes only.

As usual in Vancouver, it was dull, cool and sprinkling light rain, but I didn't care. I was home. I stepped down the ramp, limping slightly, and pushed through the barrier. It didn't take long for Customs to release me and then I was out in the waiting room, looking around for my wife. There was the Chief, coming for me with a big smile. I grabbed his hand, glad to see him.

"Where's Pat?"

"In the hospital, having that baby of yours." He laughed at my startled expression. "There's nothing to worry about."

"Nothing to worry about! My God! Let's get going!"

In the car we didn't talk much. At last he pulled into his own parking space at the Lab and turned to me.

"Get on over to the Labor Room and see Pat. I'll meet you up in my office later."

I almost ran to the big Maternity Building, close by, and stepped into the elevator. At the desk of Delivery, the nurse stood up in protest.

"I'm sorry. You can't come in here."

I explained hurriedly who I was.

"Why of course, Doctor," she said. "Here's a gown and mask...but hurry...she's well into the second stage now."

I pushed open the door of Delivery Room number three. The doctor looked around and his eyes widened in surprise above the mask as he recognized me. It was Ray Thorne.

"Pat, look who's here!" he said.

Her hair was wet and her upper lip moist from the strain and the warmth of the room. I bent over her and her eyes were big as she recognized me.

"Darling, you got here! You got here just in time!"

In that highly emotional moment she was not her usual stoical self. She began to cry. I dropped my mask. The hell with so-called sterile technique! These bugs were all in the family. I kissed her. She smiled even though a hard pain was beginning.

"Now it will be all right," she whispered.

I hung on to her hand and looked up at the mirror that pictured the other end of the delivery table.

"Push hard now," Ray said, as the baby's head came down. She strained and gasped, her face reddened with effort.

"OK, I've got it...easy now...easy now," Ray was saying.

Her mouth opened as if to scream but no sound came.

"Gently does it. Don't push any more."

She squeezed down on my hand and the nails bit into me. I stroked her head. Her body tensed with one last spasm and then I heard the suction going as the baby gasped. She loosened her grip and went limp.

"It's a boy...a boy!" Ray shouted, his eyes twinkling with pleasure over the mask as he held the child up by the feet. The sharp wail of my first-born son was loud in the room. I put my face down to Pat as she cried for joy.

Back in the Laboratory I passed by the offices until I came to the electron microscope room. Polly was busy setting up for a picture but turned at the noise.

"John, darling! Oh, I'm so happy to see you." She came over to me, put her hands on my shoulders and kissed me.

"Have you seen Pat yet? But of course you have. How is she? Has she had that baby yet?"

"Yes I have. She's doing fine. It's a boy."

"Wonderful!" she exclaimed, and kissed me again. "That's for good luck," she explained. "You three will make such a nice family." Her smile faded as the sun goes behind a cloud and for an instant her eyes, though still on my face, seemed to look far away beyond me into infinity.

"And what about you Polly?" I said quietly.

"Harry's dead!" she said abruptly, her mouth held firm to still the trembling of her chin.

"God! No!" I reached out and took her hands. "Polly!" I shook my head. I couldn't think of a thing to say. She took a deep breath and tried to relax, to shake off whatever terrible picture she had imagined of his ending.

"Pat tells me she wrote to you about Harry getting to the Chinese mainland," she said at last.

"Yes, I knew he was there but the last word I had before we dropped into Korea was that they were making good progress in their research."

"They were for a while," she said sadly, "but one day the Communists found out about it and threw a surprise attack at them. They were driven back to the beach and Harry was hit in the head with a piece of shrapnel. The Nationalists managed to get them away to Taiwan and they turned him over to the Americans. He died in Taipei."

"Do you know what killed him?" I asked.

"Some sort of fungus disease of the brain that entered through the wound. He was never fully conscious after he got hit. He didn't rally from the operation but just gradually weakened and died."

"How did you find out?"

"One of the officers who was with him on the mainland wrote to me."

She stopped talking and, in the silence, a dripping tap counted away the seconds. Her eyes were full of tears now.

"The thing that bothers me a whole lot," she said, "he died among strangers, all alone."

"He fought for freedom, Polly," I said. "He had company."

"I'm sorry John," she took my hand again. "I forget other people in my own selfish worries." She wiped away the tears. "Did you lose many men in your unit?"

"Eight killed out of thirty…and a few more wounded; one died of the bleeding death. We were lucky compared to some of the other Ranger teams I hear."

"We don't know much about these things," she said. "The papers talk of the hidden war in a vague sort of way but nobody has come right out with it yet."

"It won't be long now," I said grimly. "I think we've got them by the short hairs." I picked up an unopened morning paper lying on the table and looked at the headline. "There you are!" I showed it to her. "Revolt Rumored in Russia!"

She looked in silence and then got up. "Let's forget war for today. Let's celebrate your homecoming and the new baby. I'm going to get George right now and we'll all go over to see that baby and Pat and then take off for the rest of the day."

"Suits me fine," I said and followed her out the door.

Six months later it was over. It wasn't much of a revolution. The Russian people had had enough of disease and famine and when the army turned over, almost to a man, to the rebels, the Reds folded up faster than the White Russians had in 1918. The United States was the only major power left in the world, in fact the only large population, since the measlepox and now the bleeding death had decimated much of Asia, Europe and South America, to say nothing of the sterilizing effects of the S-Flu. It would take months or years to eradicate all breeding places of these pests from the earth and when it was over there would be plenty of room for everybody; no more squabbles about territory; no more delusions of world empire; those who were left would be too busy trying to keep running what businesses and factories, ships and planes they already had, without wanting more.

This was a new world, a strange world full of problems. Better that the sorrows of the past be put away and a fresh beginning made.

THE END

If you've enjoyed this book, you will not want to miss these terrific titles…

ARMCHAIR SCI-FI, FANTASY, & HORROR DOUBLE NOVELS, $12.95 *each*

D-1   **THE GALAXY RAIDERS** by William P. McGivern
    SPACE STATION #1 by Frank Belknap Long

D-2   **THE PROGRAMMED PEOPLE** by Jack Sharkey
    SLAVES OF THE CRYSTAL BRAIN by William Carter Sawtelle

D-3   **YOU'RE ALL ALONE** by Fritz Leiber
    THE LIQUID MAN by Bernard C. Gilford

D-4   **CITADEL OF THE STAR LORDS** by Edmund Hamilton
    VOYAGE TO ETERNITY by Milton Lesser

D-5   **IRON MEN OF VENUS** by Don Wilcox
    THE MAN WITH ABSOLUTE MOTION by Noel Loomis

D-6   **WHO SOWS THE WIND...** by Rog Phillips
    THE PUZZLE PLANET by Robert A. W. Lowndes

D-7   **PLANET OF DREAD** by Murray Leinster
    TWICE UPON A TIME by Charles L. Fontenay

D-8   **THE TERROR OUT OF SPACE** by Dwight V. Swain
    QUEST OF THE GOLDEN APE by Ivar Jorgensen and Adam Chase

D-9   **SECRET OF MARRACOTT DEEP** by Henry Slesar
    PAWN OF THE BLACK FLEET by Mark Clifton.

D-10   **BEYOND THE RINGS OF SATURN** by Robert Moore Williams
    A MAN OBSESSED by Alan E. Nourse

ARMCHAIR SCIENCE FICTION CLASSICS, $12.95 each

C-1   **THE GREEN MAN**
    by Harold M. Sherman

C-2   **A TRACE OF MEMORY**
    By Keith Laumer

C-3   **INTO PLUTONIAN DEPTHS**
    by Stanton A. Coblentz

ARMCHAIR MASTERS OF SCIENCE FICTION SERIES, $16.95 each

M-1   **MASTERS OF SCIENCE FICTION, Vol. One**
    Bryce Walton—"Dark of the Moon" and other tales

M-2   **MASTERS OF SCIENCE FICTION, Vol. Two**
    Jerome Bixby: "One Way Street" and other tales

If you've enjoyed this book, you will not want to miss these terrific titles…

ARMCHAIR SCI-FI & HORROR DOUBLE NOVELS, $12.95 each

D-11   **PERIL OF THE STARMEN** by Kris Neville
        THE STRANGE INVASION by Murray Leinster

D-12   **THE STAR LORD** by Boyd Ellanby
        CAPTIVES OF THE FLAME by Samuel R. Delaney

D-13   **MEN OF THE MORNING STAR** by Edmund Hamilton
        PLANET FOR PLUNDER by Hal Clement and Sam Merwin, Jr.

D-14   **ICE CITY OF THE GORGON** by Chester S. Geier and Richard Shaver
        WHEN THE WORLD TOTTERED by Lester Del Rey

D-15   **WORLDS WITHOUT END** by Clifford D. Simak
        THE LAVENDER VINE OF DEATH by Don Wilcox

D-16   **SHADOW ON THE MOON** by Joe Gibson
        ARMAGEDDON EARTH by Geoff St. Reynard

D-17   **THE GIRL WHO LOVED DEATH** by Paul W. Fairman
        SLAVE PLANET by Laurence M. Janifer

D-18   **SECOND CHANCE** by J. F. Bone
        MISSION TO A DISTANT STAR by Frank Belknap Long

D-19   **THE SYNDIC** by C. M. Kornbluth
        FLIGHT TO FOREVER by Poul Anderson

D-20   **SOMEWHERE I'LL FIND YOU** by Milton Lesser
        THE TIME ARMADA by Fox B. Holden

ARMCHAIR SCIENCE FICTION CLASSICS, $12.95 each

C-4   **CORPUS EARTHLING**
       by Louis Charbonneau

C-5   **THE TIME DISSOLVER**
       by Jerry Sohl

C-6   **WEST OF THE SUN**
       by Edgar Pangborn

ARMCHAIR SCIENCE FICTION & HORROR GEMS SERIES, $12.95 each

G-1   **SCIENCE FICTION GEMS, Vol. One**
       Isaac Asimov and others

G-2   **HORROR GEMS, Vol. One**
       Carl Jacobi and others

If you've enjoyed this book, you will not want to miss these terrific titles…

ARMCHAIR SCI-FI, FANTASY, & HORROR DOUBLE NOVELS, $12.95 each

D-21 **EMPIRE OF EVIL** by Robert Arnette
THE SIGN OF THE TIGER by Alan E. Nourse & J. A. Meyer

D-22 **OPERATION SQUARE PEG** by Frank Belknap Long
ENCHANTRESS OF VENUS by Leigh Brackett

D-23 **THE LIFE WATCH** by Lester Del Rey
CREATURES OF THE ABYSS by Murray Leinster

D-24 **LEGION OF LAZARUS** by Edmond Hamilton
STAR HUNTER by Andre Norton

D-25 **EMPIRE OF WOMEN** by John Fletcher
ONE OF OUR CITIES IS MISSING by Irving Cox

D-26 **THE WRONG SIDE OF PARADISE** by Raymond F. Jones
THE INVOLUNTARY IMMORTALS by Rog Phillips

D-27 **EARTH QUARTER** by Damon Knight
ENVOY TO NEW WORLDS by Keith Laumer

D-28 **SLAVES TO THE METAL HORDE** by Milton Lesser
HUNTERS OUT OF TIME by Joseph E. Kelleam

D-29 **RX JUPITER SAVE US** by Ward Moore
BEWARE THE USURPERS by Geoff St. Reynard

D-30 **SECRET OF THE SERPENT** by Don Wilcox
CRUSADE ACROSS THE VOID by Dwight V. Swain

ARMCHAIR SCIENCE FICTION CLASSICS, $12.95 each

C-7 **THE SHAVER MYSTERY, pt. 1**
by Richard S. Shaver

C-8 **THE SHAVER MYSTERY, pt. 2**
by Richard S. Shaver

C-9 **MURDER IN SPACE** by David V. Reed
by David V. Reed

ARMCHAIR MASTERS OF SCIENCE FICTION SERIES, $16.95 each

M-3 **MASTERS OF SCIENCE FICTION, Vol. Three**
Robert Sheckley, "The Perfect Woman" and other tales

M-4 **MASTERS OF SCIENCE FICTION, Vol. Four**
Mack Reynolds, "Stowaway" and other tales

If you've enjoyed this book, you will not want to miss these terrific titles...

ARMCHAIR SCI-FI & HORROR DOUBLE NOVELS, $12.95 each

D-31   **A HOAX IN TIME** by Keith Laumer
       INSIDE EARTH by Poul Anderson

D-32   **TERROR STATION** by Dwight V. Swain
       THE WEAPON FROM ETERNITY by Dwight V. Swain

D-33   **THE SHIP FROM INFINITY** by Edmond Hamilton
       TAKEOFF by C. M. Kornbluth

D-34   **THE METAL DOOM** by David H. Keller
       TWELVE TIMES ZERO by Howard Browne

D-35   **HUNTERS OUT OF SPACE** by Joseph Kelleam
       INVASION FROM THE DEEP by Paul W. Fairman,

D-36   **THE BEES OF DEATH** by Robert Moore Williams
       A PLAGUE OF PYTHONS by Frederick Pohl

D-37   **THE LORDS OF QUARMALL** by Fritz Leiber and Harry Fischer
       BEACON TO ELSEWHERE by James H. Schmitz

D-38   **BEYOND PLUTO** by John S. Campbell
       ARTERY OF FIRE by Thomas N. Scortia

D-39   **SPECIAL DELIVERY** by Kris Neville
       NO TIME FOR TOFFEE by Charles F. Meyers

D-40   **RECALLED TO LIFE** by Robert Silverberg
       JUNGLE IN THE SKY by Milton Lesser

ARMCHAIR SCIENCE FICTION CLASSICS, $12.95 each

C-10   **MARS IS MY DESTINATION**
       by Frank Belknap Long

C-11   **SPACE PLAGUE**
       by George O. Smith

C-12   **SO SHALL YE REAP**
       by Rog Phillips

ARMCHAIR SCIENCE FICTION & HORROR GEMS SERIES, $12.95 each

G-3   **SCIENCE FICTION GEMS, Vol. Two**
      James Blish and others

G-4   **HORROR GEMS, Vol. Two**
      Joseph Payne Brennan and others

If you've enjoyed this book, you will not want to miss these terrific titles...

ARMCHAIR SCI-FI & HORROR DOUBLE NOVELS, $12.95 each

D-41 **FULL CYCLE** by Clifford D. Simak
IT WAS THE DAY OF THE ROBOT by Frank Belknap Long

D-42 **THIS CROWDED EARTH** by Robert Bloch
REIGN OF THE TELEPUPPETS by Daniel Galouye

D-43 **THE CRISPIN AFFAIR** by Jack Sharkey
THE RED HELL OF JUPITER by Paul Ernst

D-44 **PLANET OF DREAD** by Dwight V. Swain
WE THE MACHINE by Gerald Vance

D-45 **THE STAR HUNTER** by Edmond Hamilton
THE ALIEN by Raymond F. Jones

D-46 **WORLD OF IF** by Rog Phillips
SLAVE RAIDERS FROM MERCURY by Don Wilcox

D-47 **THE ULTIMATE PERIL** by Robert Abernathy
PLANET OF SHAME by Bruce Elliot

D-48 **THE FLYING EYES** by J. Hunter Holly
SOME FABULOUS YONDER by Phillip Jose Farmer

D-49 **THE COSMIC BUNGLARS** by Geoff St. Reynard
THE BUTTONED SKY by Geoff St. Reynard

D-50 **TYRANTS OF TIME** by Milton Lesser
PARIAH PLANET by Murray Leinster

ARMCHAIR SCIENCE FICTION CLASSICS, $12.95 each

C-13 **SUNKEN WORLD**
by Stanton A. Coblentz

C-14 **THE LAST VIAL**
by Sam McClatchie, M. D.

C-15 **WE WHO SURVIVED (THE FIFTH ICE AGE)**
by Sterling Noel

ARMCHAIR MASTERS OF SCIENCE FICTION SERIES, $16.95 each

MS-5 **MASTERS OF SCIENCE FICTION, Vol. Five**
Winston K. Marks—Test Colony and other classics

MS-6 **MASTERS OF SCIENCE FICTION, Vol. Six**
Fritz Leiber—Deadly Moon and other classics

www.ingramcontent.com/pod-product-compliance
Lightning Source LLC
Chambersburg PA
CBHW030326180626
46810CB00003B/1236